DINGO'S RECOVERY

Genevieve Fortin

BELLA
BOOKS

2018

Bella Books, Inc.
P.O. Box 10543
Tallahassee, FL 32302

Printed in the United States of America on acid-free paper.

First Bella Books Edition 2018

Editor: Medora MacDougall
Cover Designer: Judith Fellows

ISBN: 978-1-59493-588-6

Other Bella Books by Genevieve Fortin

First Fall
Two Kinds of Elizabeth
Water's Edge

Acknowledgments

They say you can find inspiration anywhere. I believe it now more than ever. When our little dog Spike injured his leg while playing in the yard with our larger dog Betty, I didn't immediately think the incident would inspire a novel. But it did. It was after two or three appointments at the veterinarian clinic that I realized the twelve-week timeframe his recovery would take might be an interesting setting for a romance novel. I'm glad I did. It gave me a chance to turn an adventure that could have been nothing but sad, stressful, and oh so costly, into something much more positive and inspiring. So the first thank-you goes to our dogs.

The second goes to the wonderful Medora MacDougall, who worked hard to make my book better, hacking down hundred of "justs" and other useless words until we were left with a much lighter, enjoyable read. It was great working with you again and I hope it won't be the last time.

I also want to thank Linda and the entire Bella Books team, for their constant support and encouragement. Thank you for working with me through my insecurities and multiple questions.

A very special thank-you goes to the young Maine artist who painted the injured Dingo used on the book cover. Zoe Walker is just seventeen years old but her talent goes well beyond her years. She's one to watch! I sure will keep following her and can't wait to see what she'll paint next.

I also want to thank Denise, my partner, who never misses a chance to remind me when it's time to write. Your support means the world to me, always.

Last but not least, thank you, dear readers. The fact that you choose my books among so many others will never be taken for granted. I write for you—and for me, of course.

About the Author

Genevieve is French Canadian but claims her heart holds dual citizenship. Not surprising since she lived in the USA for thirteen years and still visits every chance she gets. Besides writing and reading, her passions include traveling, decadent desserts, fruity martinis, and watching HGTV. For now she lives in St-Georges, just a few miles north of the border between Maine and Quebec. She and her partner share a house with their two dogs, Spike and Betty.

Dedication

For Denise, in memory of the first Tanzania Raspberry chocolate truffle we shared.

CHAPTER ONE

"If making this drive every day doesn't show you I love you, I don't know what will," Joyce Allen said to her basenji, squinting at him through the rearview mirror of her Subaru Forester. Safely anchored to the backseat with his harness and seat belt, Dingo cocked his head at his owner in reply. Joyce grinned at the familiar, quizzical expression the wrinkles on his forehead created.

She often complained about having to drive across town to the Bangor dog park while her own house was located right next to another of the city's multiple green spaces. Unfortunately, Saxl Park didn't have an enclosed area dedicated to dogs, and letting Dingo run free without physical boundaries to keep him from chasing after any squirrel, cat, or inanimate object blown by the wind was a sport Joyce had quickly learned she didn't enjoy at all. He was a talented little escape artist and she was not quite as talented at catching him. Seeing him run freely and play with other dogs within the security of a fenced-in park, however, was an enjoyable sight. And it was well worth the drive. She would never admit it to Dingo, of course.

"I hope you remember this tonight when I want to sleep and you'd rather practice your vocalization exercises. You'll never make the Met, you know. So give it up, little brat. Will you?"

Like all basenjis, Dingo didn't bark but made a whiny yodel that Joyce found amusing and charming—until eleven at night. At that time Joyce wished her furry companion came with an "off" button, but instead that was the exact time his yodel got louder and more annoying. After a year of sharing her home and life with the red and white little beast, however, their sleeping time was the only matter Joyce and Dingo didn't agree on. The rest of their days went by in almost perfect harmony.

Joyce turned right on Watchmaker Street, parked in front of the familiar three fenced-in areas and turned the rearview mirror so she could retouch her makeup. She wished she didn't need to worry so much about her appearance when she went to the dog park. Of all places, the park should have been the haven where she could wear yoga pants and an old sweatshirt without worrying about being judged, she mused with frustration. But experience had taught her that her sister's snooty friends or those of her late wife were everywhere in Bangor. And they all knew each other. Joyce wished she didn't care what they might or might not say about her, but she did.

Of course, Evelyn's friends had been her friends too until Evelyn was taken away by a brain tumor three years ago, but their friendship with Joyce had faded after Evelyn's death. Joyce had been saddened by their distant disposition at first, when she most needed them, but now she didn't miss them and she wished she wouldn't have to worry about meeting them every time she left the house.

Joyce used her fingertips to fluff her thick silver hair, cut above her shoulders, and granted herself a satisfied smile. She'd quit coloring her hair during the eighteen-month depression she'd sunk into after she'd lost Evelyn and she'd never started again. Her silver hair had a bright, lustrous quality that was the envy of women her age and made her look more elegant and sophisticated rather than older.

The last mirror check was directed to the light blue silk scarf around her neck and she twitched it into place, making sure it covered the delicate, crepe-cotton skin of her neck. Scarves were part of her signature look, fashionable yes, but chosen more for their function. At fifty-six, she didn't mind wearing a sleeveless top that left her yoga-toned arms exposed. But she would never be caught without a scarf around her neck, even in the heat of July. Satisfied with her appearance at last, she got out of her car, grabbed her purse, and opened the back door to clip Dingo's leash to his collar. Even the short distance between the car and the gate to the park, maybe twenty feet, was too risky not to use a leash on him. The dog started walking proudly by her side, his tail tightly curled on his back.

Together they entered the park for dogs weighing twenty-five pounds or more and as soon as she closed the gate behind them, she unclipped his leash and laughed as she watched him take off like a space rocket. He ran around the park twice, as fast as he could, before he finally went to greet Slipper, a Bernese mountain dog he often played with. Dingo barely made the twenty-five pound minimum for this particular enclosed area, but he'd never seemed intimidated by much larger dogs like Slipper.

Joyce greeted Slipper's owner, Mr. Davis, with a polite nod. He was a tall and massive middle-aged man who seemed friendly enough but kept to himself. Joyce was grateful he and his dog were the only souls in sight at nine a.m. on this beautiful Friday morning. She wasn't in the mood to socialize. She took a deep breath of the warm air which she knew would become suffocating in a few hours and walked to the bench nearby where she spent most of her time while Dingo ran and played to his heart's content.

Joyce sat down and reached into her large purse to grab the book she was currently reading, *My Brilliant Career* by Miles Franklin. It was the story of a young woman in 1890s rural Australia and she was enthralled by it. When her love for reading had finally been revived after her depression, she'd focused on books set in Australia. She'd been drawn to the country down under ever since she'd read *The Thorn Birds* by Colleen

McCullough as a teenager. She'd fantasized about living on the large sheep station with Meggie Cleary, the beautiful girl with red-gold hair. Joyce's recovery from depression had been greatly helped by rekindling old dreams she'd forgotten during her twenty-eight-year relationship with Evelyn. Old dreams like visiting Australia, a trip that was now on her bucket list and that she planned on making sooner rather than later.

When she'd decided to get a dog, she'd researched breeds over the Internet until she'd seen a picture of a basenji. The dog's red and white hair, its large erect ears, and its inquisitive expression had reminded her of a miniature version of a dingo, the infamous wild dog found in Australian deserts and grasslands. She'd fallen in love with that picture and had decided there and then that the basenji was the right breed for her. Of course she'd learned later while researching breeders that basenjis came from Africa and didn't have anything in common with dingoes, but that didn't keep her from finding and adopting her own little Dingo.

Joyce had read two pages of her book when she heard a screeching yelp she recognized as Dingo's. The loud, high-pitched sound was followed by a deep and panicked, "Oh my god." Joyce looked up and saw Dingo on the ground. Mr. Davis was on his knees by his side. Her heart briefly stopped at the sight before it started racing. She dropped her book on the bench and ran to Dingo's side.

She didn't have time to ask what had happened before Mr. Davis recounted the entire event in a trembling voice. "They were just running and playing like they usually do. Then Dingo stopped for some reason and Slipper ran over him. I think he ran right up Dingo's back leg. Poor dog. I'm so sorry."

"There's nothing to be sorry about. It was obviously an accident. I know Slipper wouldn't hurt Dingo on purpose." Joyce's statement was meant to appease Mr. Davis, but her own throat tightened as she caressed Dingo's side and she knew her facial expression didn't match her reassuring words. She was beyond scared.

"Can you get up, little brat?" she asked Dingo in a low, soothing voice as she clicked her fingers together over his head, inviting him to stand up. He got on his feet, but immediately lifted his left back leg and kept it bent against his belly, refusing to put any weight on it. "Something's wrong with your leg, huh?" She started rubbing and manipulating his entire body, starting with his neck. Nothing seemed to hurt until she attempted to stretch his left back leg and Dingo snapped at her before he whimpered faintly. She jerked her hand out of his reach. He'd never snapped at anybody before. "That hurts, doesn't it?"

"I think you better take him to the vet," Mr. Davis said with grief. "I'll pay the bill. Anything he needs."

"Nonsense. It's not your fault. I won't accept your money, but I think you're right about the vet." Joyce started gathering Dingo in her arms, but Mr. Davis stopped her.

"Let me. I'll take him to your car for you."

Joyce knew she was perfectly able to carry her own dog, but Mr. Davis needed to help in some way so she let him carry Dingo. As she moved to stand up, she felt a wet tongue on her cheek and turned to face Slipper, who looked as sorry as his owner was. "Don't worry, Slipper. It's not your fault you're such a big boy. Dingo will be fine." She petted Slipper's head and stopped by the bench to gather her book and purse before she followed Mr. Davis and Dingo to her car.

Alone in her vehicle with Dingo sitting and whimpering in the backseat, Joyce didn't have anyone left to reassure about his condition except herself, but she was much less successful than she'd been with Mr. Davis and Slipper. She kept glancing at him through the rearview mirror. The wrinkles on his forehead that usually made him look curious made him appear so sad now. It was heartbreaking. She could hardly breathe as panic settled in and caused her airways to tighten up. What if his leg was broken beyond repair? Worse, what if he had internal injuries Joyce couldn't see? Slipper had to weigh over a hundred pounds. If he'd run on Dingo's body he might have caused a lot of damage. Maybe Mr. Davis hadn't seen everything. Joyce couldn't lose Dingo.

Joyce had grown up in a house where dogs were part of the family and she'd always thought she'd have a dog of her own as an adult. Evelyn had never wanted a dog. She'd met Evelyn not long after she'd started working at the Bangor Savings Bank, and they'd started to live together shortly after. Evelyn didn't have allergies, but she didn't want animals in her home. She claimed they were too messy in a house and made traveling too complicated. They'd have to find a sitter before they went anywhere overnight. Hell, even if they simply went out to dinner they'd have to be back at a certain time to walk and feed the dog. It was a responsibility Evelyn didn't want to take on. Joyce had argued at first but finally had given up. She'd almost forgotten about her need for canine companionship until she'd come out of her depression. She'd realized that owning a dog was another dream she'd put aside during their relationship. She'd fulfilled the first of those dreams when she'd adopted Dingo.

Joyce took another look at Dingo, leaning on his right side to protect his injured leg. She smiled at him as tears threatened her vision and focused back on the road.

Evelyn Graham had been a wonderful life partner. She was kind, generous, ambitious, and Joyce had been happy with her. Evelyn Graham was also a born leader. She'd taken the lead in every single aspect of her life and it had been natural for her to take the reins in their relationship as well. Joyce, easy-going by nature, had let her make all the important decisions and she didn't regret it. Evelyn's decisions had been wise and had allowed them to build a comfortable life as a couple. They'd worked together at the Bangor Savings Bank, climbing the corporate ladder until Joyce became marketing director and Evelyn a VP of finance. They had a beautiful home in a sought-after neighborhood where they often entertained their friends. Joyce had indeed been happy with Evelyn. She'd been lost when she'd passed away.

Then, slowly, the dark veil that Evelyn's death had thrown over Joyce's life had started to rise, and she'd realized she couldn't keep being Evelyn's Joyce. That Joyce had existed within the confinement of their life as a couple, but she couldn't exist anymore. She had the conviction that her essence had been buried deep inside her during those twenty-eight years. She wasn't sure how or when it had happened, but she knew it had.

She didn't blame Evelyn for her losing herself and she didn't regret loving and living with Evelyn, but now she wanted to reconnect with her true self. It would be a long process, but she had to start somewhere. So she'd taken the first two steps toward that goal a year ago. She'd retired from her job at the Bangor Savings Bank, and then she'd adopted Dingo.

She couldn't lose him. He was too big a part of the new life she was building, not to mention being her closest friend and ally in a quest she hadn't shared with anyone but him. She simply couldn't lose him.

"Let's go in and get you all better," she whispered with determination as she took him into her arms and walked into the Perry Veterinary Clinic.

CHAPTER TWO

Amanda Carter enjoyed working at the Perry Veterinary Clinic. She'd been happy at the Maine Veterinary Medical Center in Scarborough, south of Portland. She'd worked there since she'd graduated from veterinary school and she'd learned much. When Douglas Perry had offered her partnership in his small clinic in Bangor, however, she hadn't hesitated. Opening her own clinic or becoming partner in an established practice was a career move she'd been planning on making. Moving to Bangor also brought her even closer to the vast forests she enjoyed exploring alone with her thoughts and her backpack. She felt more at home in nature than in any other place and nature was everywhere around this town.

She hadn't known Doug well when he'd made the offer. She'd met him in a professional conference and they'd bonded as the two most reserved people attending the event. They found they had similar practices and beliefs and after the convention, they'd called each other several times to ask for advice on complicated cases. When Doug found himself overwhelmed with the rapid growth of his clinic, he'd asked her to join him as a partner.

Amanda still didn't know Doug all that well even though she'd been working at the clinic for a little over a month now. In fact, all she knew about him was that he had a wife and a son she would guess to be about eight or nine years old. Not that he'd talked about them. She'd seen the family picture sitting on his cluttered desk. That minuscule window into Doug's private life was still a lot more than he knew about her own life outside of work. That was the way she wanted it. They seemed to be in silent agreement, in fact, that the only thing it was necessary for them to talk to each other about was their patients' needs.

He didn't know, for example, that today was her birthday. This year the seventh of July would go by without awkward hugs or kisses, without cake that would go to waste, without a gift she might have to return to the store.

Amanda wasn't made for embarrassing social settings of those sorts. And neither was Doug. They were made for sevenths of July like today, their schedules filled with yearly exams, routine vaccinations, spaying and neutering, and three emergencies. They'd managed to handle two of them, but one they'd had to refer to an emergency veterinary hospital because the clinic was not equipped for surgeries that complicated. And all of that before eleven a.m. on a Friday. They didn't have time for birthdays.

Amanda entered Exam Room Number Three. It was her favorite of the four examination rooms because of the large poster displayed on one of its beige walls between ads for flea and tick control treatments. The poster showed a gigantic Great Dane looking down on a tiny Chihuahua, with the caption "Never be afraid to say what you really feel." The caption was appropriate for a vet practice, but Amanda smiled every time she saw it because someone, probably Doug, had covered the other caption. She'd seen the poster somewhere else and knew that underneath the white correction fluid on this print were words that revealed what the Chihuahua really felt—"Fuck off." The perfect Chihuahua thing to say, she thought. When she entered the exam room today, however, she didn't even look at the poster.

Her attention was immediately captured by the woman standing by the exam table where a basenji sat, held in trembling hands. She was touched by the woman's obvious affection for her animal and the sincere concern she saw in her eyes, but those were qualities she'd seen a million times before in her career.

There was something else about her. Something in her eyes and overall presence. She was a strikingly beautiful, stylish, mature woman, but that couldn't be the only thing that was keeping Amanda's gaze on her. Not even Professor Jones, on whom she'd had a powerful and long-lasting crush when she was studying veterinary medicine, had affected her this way. A warm tingling energy coursed through her body, as if this woman, this incarnation of grace and beauty, had been sent to her for reasons she couldn't explain yet. As if the universe had sent her a birthday present she hadn't known she wanted.

"Doctor Carter, this is Ms. Allen," Isabelle explained from the other side of the exam table, "and this here is Dingo. Dingo had a little accident in the park and injured his leg."

The spell she was under having been broken by the vet tech's voice, Amanda turned to face her and nodded, hoping she hadn't been staring at Ms. Allen too long before Isabelle intervened. She then turned back to Ms. Allen and extended her hand, willing it not to tremble. "Nice to meet you, Ms. Allen. Doctor Amanda Carter. I'll be examining Dingo today."

"Nice to meet you, Doctor. Please fix him, will you?"

Ms. Allen shook Amanda's hand and the contact sent another wave of unfamiliar and unexplained electricity through her veins. It took every ounce of self-control she possessed to keep her composure. She'd never been nervous in an exam room before. She'd never felt out of control. Never been so aware of her Caribbean blue scrubs under her white lab coat and of her boring ponytail. She'd always been businesslike, the ever-efficient, calm, and collected Doctor Carter. She had to be that person again now. For Ms. Allen and for Dingo. She took a deep breath, pushed her glasses back up the bridge of her nose with her index finger, and started examining Dingo.

She carefully avoided glancing at Dingo's owner as she took his temperature, listened to his heart, and probed his entire body with the help of Isabelle, who was holding him. Ms. Allen stood at the end of the exam table, whispering words of encouragement to the dog. Her voice was low and soothing and though it was helping Dingo remain calm, it was having the opposite effect on Amanda, who thought she could feel the woman's breath and the vibration of her voice on the skin of her arms and hands as she went on with the examination.

Somehow Amanda was able to go through every step of her thorough checkup. She cleared her throat before she spoke in an attempt to calm her nerves. "The good news is that nothing else seems to be wrong with Dingo," she said without looking at the woman. "Something is definitely wrong with his leg though. We'll need to take X-rays to know exactly what the problem is."

"I see. Yes, that makes sense. Do you think it's bad, Doctor?"

Amanda heard the distress in her voice and couldn't resist looking at her and offering an encouraging smile this time when she spoke. "Don't worry. We'll most likely be able to get Dingo back running as if nothing had ever happened." The sigh of relief she heard come out of Ms. Allen made her realize she hadn't been breathing that well either. She couldn't resist inhaling and exhaling deeply.

Amanda had never been good with people, but she'd loved animals all of her life and she hated seeing them suffer. She'd never had a pet of her own as a child because of the unpredictable nature of her home and didn't have one now because she didn't spend enough time at home and she didn't think it'd be fair, but she could still imagine how bad the pain must be when the animal that was suffering was a part of your family. She'd always been able to relate to that anguish, but she'd never felt it in such a physical, almost symbiotic way as she was now.

"Dingo is young and I'm convinced he'll recover," she continued. "The question now is what will need to be done to get him there. The X-rays will tell us if we can fix him here with a splint that will hold his leg in place while he recovers, or if he'll need to go to Brewer's Veterinary Hospital for surgery."

"Oh my god," Ms. Allen exclaimed, alarmed by the possibility of surgery.

Amanda instinctively covered the woman's hand with her own to reassure her. She'd seen similar reactions in clients who panicked thinking of the cost a surgery could represent, and she understood them. Some people simply didn't have thousands of dollars to pay for their pet's surgery. She had a feeling, however, that paying for surgery wouldn't be a problem for Dingo's owner. Amanda didn't know much about fashion, but she guessed the fancy clothes Ms. Allen had worn to the dog park hadn't come from Walmart. The luxurious light blue scarf she was wearing probably cost more on its own than Amanda's entire outfit. No, money was certainly not the issue. Ms. Allen's concern was more likely about the process and the pain Dingo would have to endure as well as the possible complications surgery entailed.

"Let's take it one step at a time, okay?" Ms. Allen nodded her understanding, so Amanda went on. "Right now we need to give Dingo a mild sedative so we can take the proper X-rays. That's the first step. It might take some time. Would you like to go home and wait for us to call you when we know more?"

"No, I'd rather stay, if you don't mind."

Amanda smiled. She would have been surprised if she'd agreed to leave the clinic without Dingo. "Of course. I understand. There is a coffee machine in the waiting room. Please take a seat and we'll call you as soon as we can take a look at the X-rays."

"Thank you," Ms. Allen said with a weak voice and the first smile Amanda had seen on her face. It was a tentative smile, still tainted with worry, but it was enough for Amanda to know she was grateful and enough for her to want nothing more than to see an even lighter, untroubled smile light up her features. A smile that Amanda would have elicited in her. She hoped she would get that chance once she looked at Dingo's X-rays.

"You're welcome. Isabelle, will you please show Ms. Allen the waiting room?"

"Yes, right this way," Isabelle answered as she opened the door and escorted her out of the exam room.

Left alone with Dingo, Amanda sighed heavily. She missed the closeness of Dingo's owner, but she was finally able to focus all of her attention on the dog. The little beast looked up at her from the exam table, panting with pain and using the wrinkles on his forehead to question her. "Don't worry, pup. I'll take good care of you. I'm not completely useless, you know."

She scratched Dingo's head affectionately and took him in her arms before she added, "You do have a lovely mommy, though, don't you?" Dingo licked Amanda's face, which she took as his way of agreeing with her assessment. She took him out of the exam room to the back of the clinic where Isabelle helped administer the sedative that would allow them to take X-rays of his injured leg.

She hoped with all of her heart that Dingo wouldn't need surgery. Part of that hope came from wanting to make things easier on him and his owner. Another, more selfish part, came from her wish to keep treating his leg at the clinic over the next few weeks, which would mean she would see his owner again. Maybe enough times to figure out what to do with that beautiful birthday present the universe had sent her.

CHAPTER THREE

"Thank you, Barb, but I can handle this on my own," Joyce declared, trying to reassure her sister over the phone as she sat in the waiting room. The last thing she needed was for Barbara to come and join her. Sadly, she couldn't trust her sister to be the source of comfort she needed in her current situation.

"It doesn't sound like you're handling it, Joyce. You're crying."

"I *was* crying, I'm fine now. See, you helped from a distance," Joyce replied, rolling her eyes and hoping the sarcasm wasn't obvious in her voice.

"I can't believe you've gone ahead and complicated your life with this animal. Now not only are you crying over his broken leg, but that whole little adventure in the park will cost you a fortune. Evelyn would never have let that happen, that's for sure."

And there it was: the real reason why Barbara would be useless in comforting her through Dingo's ordeal. She hated the idea of owning a dog or any kind of pet even more than Evelyn had. Her disdain for animals made it hard to believe they'd been raised in the same home. She'd tried to dissuade Joyce from adopting a dog from the time she'd learned about her plans until the very morning she'd gone to pick up her puppy. What Joyce needed now was someone who would sympathize with the pain and anxiety she was going through because Dingo was injured, not someone who would go on and on about why she should never have burdened herself with a dog in the first place.

"Listen, I really don't need this right now. Evelyn is dead. She can't keep me from having a dog anymore and neither can you. I live my own life now. And my life includes a dog named Dingo. I love him and he's injured and I'll cry over that as long as I want to, damn it! I'm going to hang up now. Do *not* come, you hear me?"

Before Barbara could answer, Joyce hung up. She hoped she hadn't raised her voice too much, but the young woman sitting across from her in the waiting room was staring at her and the Maltese sitting on the woman's lap growled at her. "Some people don't get it, do they?" she said to the woman, hoping to elicit her compassion.

"Oh, I know what you mean. This one here is my baby," the woman replied as she scratched her Maltese's neck. Joyce smiled at her as her heart broke thinking of how her own sister had been incapable of giving her the support this stranger had managed to offer with one simple comment. She dropped her cell phone into the depths of her purse and got up from her seat to go make herself a second cup of coffee.

She didn't like the fact that she'd been forced to speak to. Barbara that way, but she was proud she'd been able to stand up to her. She'd had a few similar outbursts recently. They were part of the process of taking back control of her own life and letting her true self come out of its shell. It wasn't easy and it left her exhausted every single time, but it was necessary. She put skim milk in her coffee and with a sigh went back to the chair she'd occupied for over an hour.

As she waited, she tried to focus on the framed art of cats and dogs that tastefully covered the walls of the waiting room and adjacent reception area of the clinic. They brightened the beige walls and proved that she was not the only person in the world who loved animals as much as she did.

She went back to the photo she'd been obsessing over since she'd sat in the waiting room. The image was of a basset hound laying his head on a bandaged front leg. Basset hounds were probably the most pitiful looking of dogs, she mused, with those sad, droopy eyes and those long, floppy ears. The dog in the frame appeared so afflicted by his injured leg. Joyce's heart tightened again as she imagined Dingo in pain. She took a deep breath and recalled Doctor Carter's reassuring words. "Let's take it one step at a time," she said, repeating the phrase to herself over and over again until she calmed down.

Joyce squirmed in her seat and pressed a hand to her aching back as she focused her thoughts on the woman caring for Dingo. She must be new in town. Doctor Perry had always examined Dingo and administered all of his routine vaccinations until today. She looked so young Joyce thought she might have just graduated from veterinary school. Her youth, however, didn't keep Joyce from instinctively trusting her with Dingo. Dingo had seemed to trust her as well, keeping still and quiet for her, something he'd never done for Doctor Perry. Doctor Carter's words had been reassuring, but even more than what she'd said, her presence had been like a soothing, enveloping coat of comfort for both Joyce and Dingo.

Joyce smiled as the image of Doctor Carter flashed in her mind. Under the professional appearance of her crisp white lab coat and dark-framed glasses, her red hair pulled back in a ponytail and the freckles on her round face betrayed the looks of a young, geeky, adorable woman. How could anyone not trust a woman like Doctor Carter? She embodied trustworthiness and credibility better than anyone Joyce had ever met before. She would take good care of Dingo. Joyce had no doubt about it. She only hoped that Dingo could remain under Doctor Carter's care and wouldn't need to transfer to Brewer for surgery.

"Ms. Allen?"

Joyce was startled by Isabelle's voice. She'd been so absorbed in her own thoughts that she hadn't noticed the vet tech approach her. Isabelle was now standing a few feet from her. Joyce turned to her. "Yes?"

"Doctor Carter will see you now, if you want to follow me."

Joyce automatically readjusted the silk scarf around her neck, grabbed her purse, and followed Isabelle, her heart racing as they walked to the exam room.

CHAPTER FOUR

"Dingo's still in the back," Amanda offered in response to the look on the face of his owner, who was obviously confused not to find her dog in the exam room.

"How is he?" she asked, furrowing her brow.

"He's doing great," Amanda said quickly to reassure her. "He behaved like a champ while we took X-rays and he's still lightly sedated as we speak. We'll take care of his leg while he's still in that relaxed state, but first I wanted to talk to you about what we'll do next." Ms. Allen nodded and Amanda realized she hadn't yet shared the information she was probably most interested in. "The good news is that he won't need surgery," she added hastily, producing an instant sigh of relief from her new favorite client.

"Oh that's really good news. Thank you, Doctor."

Amanda had hoped the time she'd spent apart from Joyce Allen would have weakened the effect the woman had on her, but as soon as the silver-haired woman entered the exam room she'd gone back to the nervous wreck she'd been earlier. She swallowed painfully, her mouth as dry as the nose of Mrs. Anderson's poodle, who suffered from severe allergies.

"So what's wrong with his leg, Doctor Carter? And what's next?" Ms. Allen asked, keeping Amanda's brain from wandering any further.

"Dingo has a sprain in his ankle. Fortunately the ligaments didn't tear. In that case he would have needed surgery. That said, the ligaments were stretched pretty badly and Dingo will need weeks to recover from his little romp in the park."

"I see," Ms. Allen said, her face falling as relief was replaced with worries about the treatment of his sprain. Amanda couldn't resist again covering her hand with her own, making every effort to bring her the comfort she needed.

"I'll be with you and Dingo through it all, Ms. Allen. You'll see it won't be that bad. What we'll do is use one of these splints to immobilize Dingo's leg." She held up a piece of translucent plastic shaped like the back leg of a dog. "We'll cut this to fit Dingo's leg perfectly, place it against his leg, and wrap it with cotton wadding and elastic tape to keep everything in place. It will be very important for Dingo not to run or jump up or off any furniture." Amanda paused and smiled at Ms. Allen, who nodded absently as she spoke. "Does Dingo sleep with you?" Amanda thought she already knew the answer to that question but still had to ask.

"Yes, he does."

Amanda offered another compassionate smile. "Of course. What I'm going to ask might be difficult, but I would recommend you keep Dingo off the bed until he's fully recovered. He could fall off the bed in the middle of the night and injure his leg. Do you have a crate or a carrier?"

"Yes, but we've never used it."

"I think you should use it for a little while. For his own safety." Amanda paused when she heard Ms. Allen sigh with discouragement. Her dark eyes shimmered with tears and Amanda's heart broke at the sight. "I know it's hard, but I promise it will be temporary. Dingo will be back in your bed soon."

"How soon?" Ms. Allen blinked several times to keep her tears from escaping and even attempted a weak smile.

"We'll keep the splint on for eight weeks. We'll need you to come back with Dingo every other week so we can change his bandage and check on his progress. Then we'll do two more weeks with just a soft bandage, no splint. And finally, two more weeks of rest without any bandage at all."

"So twelve weeks in total?"

"Yes. That's correct. Like I said, I'll be with you every step of the way."

"And then he'll be back to normal?"

"I do expect a full recovery. It will be a long process, but it will be worth it," Amanda said reassuringly as she smiled at Ms. Allen. The smile the older woman offered in return contained more hope this time.

"It could have been worse, I guess," she said almost in a whisper. Amanda admired the way she tried to see the positive in her situation.

"Much worse," Amanda confirmed. "If the ligaments had been torn, Dingo would have needed painful surgery and might never have recovered entirely. Now all he needs is some TLC from you and me for the next few weeks. We'll spoil him so much he won't even realize he's hurt."

At Ms. Allen's low chuckle, Amanda continued, "I know we both wish Dingo had never been injured in the first place, but all things considered we've been extremely lucky. Maybe the universe didn't want us to have too difficult of a time on my birthday, after all."

She laughed nervously. She'd meant to be positive and encouraging, but she'd never meant to become so personal. She was shocked at her use of "we" and "us," as if Dingo's accident had affected her as much as the elegant woman she'd do anything to comfort. As if she and Ms. Allen were going to get through Dingo's recovery together.

She was even more stunned that she'd revealed the fact that today was her birthday to a complete stranger. Isabelle, who was standing by Ms. Allen, seemed just as surprised, her eyes opening wide at Amanda's revelation. Amanda's words seemed to have the desired effect on Ms. Allen, however, and that's what mattered most to Amanda. Seeing her smile expand and her facial features relax was worth blowing her cover.

"Well, happy birthday, Doctor Carter."

"Thank you, but please call me Amanda," Amanda offered, surprising herself again. "We'll see each other a lot in the next few weeks and I'd feel more comfortable if we dropped the formalities," she added to explain a request she'd never made before.

"All right. If you'll call me Joyce."

Amanda hesitated but conceded with a nod. "Okay. Isabelle and I will go wrap that leg up now, Joyce, and we'll bring Dingo back in a few minutes."

"Wait, so your birthday is on the seventh of July?" Joyce interrupted, as if she'd come to an important realization.

"That's right," Amanda answered, wondering why Joyce was asking but enjoying the curiosity in her eyes. Joyce Allen was showing interest in her as a person rather than a doctor for the first time since they'd met earlier that day. She'd never liked being the subject of anyone's interest before. Joyce was different. She wanted to be seen by Joyce.

"Double seven. The Seeker," Joyce declared as she studied Amanda's features and finally focused on her eyes. Joyce's stare was so warm, so intense that Amanda wouldn't have been surprised if Joyce had seen her very soul. "That makes sense," Joyce concluded. Amanda guessed her expression must have shown the complete confusion she was experiencing because Joyce laughed and explained, "Sorry. I took a class in numerology last year. I'm a double three. Third of March."

"And what is that?" Joyce looked as confused as Amanda had been a few seconds before. "If the double seven makes me The Seeker, what does the double three make you?"

"Oh. The Creative Child." Joyce blushed a very light shade of pink that made her entire face glow. Grace inhabited her even when she blushed, Amanda thought. Unlike her, whose cheeks were probably sporting deep red, uneven marks at that moment.

"Interesting. Maybe you can tell me more about all of this numerology stuff when we meet again in two weeks?"

"I'll be happy to, although I'm not an expert. I simply picked up a few things, like the double digits," Joyce confirmed before Amanda and Isabelle left the exam room to tend to Dingo.

As she started adjusting his splint, Amanda was no longer certain what type of meeting was to take place in two weeks. It couldn't be a simple appointment to change a bandage. She wouldn't be looking forward to it that much if that's all it was. *Yet that's exactly what it is, dimwit, so get a hold of yourself*, she thought.

CHAPTER FIVE

Joyce carried Dingo into the house and put him on the orthopedic, ridiculously expensive dog bed she'd bought to place in the living room in an effort to keep the cream leather of her sofas clean and safe of scratches. Dingo had slept the entire way back from the clinic, feeling the effects of the pain medication Amanda had given him, and he went back to sleep almost as soon as his body touched the comfy, charcoal fleece covering his bed. She sighed again as she stared at the black elastic tape wrapped around Dingo's back leg. She smiled at the small red water hydrant sticker decorating the side of the bandage. *Nice touch*.

Amanda had been so compassionate and thoughtful she'd put a huge reassuring Band-Aid on their entire misadventure. Now that Joyce was alone with her injured basenji, however, she felt overwhelmed by the events of the day. Not to mention exhausted. Amanda had sent her home with pain medication to give Dingo every morning and every night and an Elizabethan collar in case he started to chew at his bandage, something he'd been too knocked out to do so far. If Barbara knew how much all of this had cost she'd have a fit, but she'd never know. It was none of her goddamned business.

Joyce took a deep breath and headed for the basement. She shook her head. "You really had to make me go down there, didn't you, little brat?" Before she'd adopted Dingo, she'd puppy proofed her home. In the process of identifying objects that could harm her puppy or that he could destroy, she'd realized how cluttered and suffocating her home was, as opposed to the clean and minimalist environment she craved. The puppy proofing had morphed into a major, frantic, but therapeutic cleaning spree. She'd been left with an uncluttered home in which she could breathe better. Except when she was forced to go to the basement, where all of the boxes she'd packed still sat and gathered dust, reminding her that she hadn't completed her task. She meant to have a garage sale and donate whatever was left after that, but she hadn't gotten to it yet, and she didn't want to be compelled to ask herself why.

She flipped on the light at the bottom of the stairs and studiously avoided looking at the labeled boxes. A few contained Evelyn's clothes, but most were filled with her late wife's multiple collections, including her decorative antique plates and antique dolls. She'd even packed a large portion of Evelyn's books, keeping only those she thought she might read later. She'd also kept the wall art they'd bought together.

She held her breath and moved through the boxes, heading toward the spot where she remembered leaving the crate she'd purchased to bring Dingo home and had never used again. The breeder and the training experts all said the crate was a great tool for housebreaking, but she figured that since she was home most of the time she didn't need it. Housebreaking Dingo had been a charm and she'd almost forgotten about the existence of this crate until today. She grabbed the handle of the crate and headed back up the stairs. She'd almost made it to the main floor when she heard the doorbell.

She was still holding the crate when she opened the front door and saw Barbara standing on her covered porch. Joyce's sister was barely a year older than she was, but she looked at least ten years older despite the fact that she, unlike Joyce, had kept coloring her hair. The fake blond coloring made her shoulder-long hair look dry and lifeless, Joyce thought. Not that she would ever say that, of course. Barbara's makeup was impeccable but couldn't cover deep wrinkles around her lips and on the sides of her eyes, wrinkles that reminded Joyce of their father. She was glad she'd taken after their mother and her face had remained mostly wrinkle-free.

She and Barbara had always been close. In fact she'd always followed her big sister's sound advice—until she'd adopted Dingo. Barbara's hate of all pets in general and of him in particular was such a mystery to Joyce that she sometimes wondered if Barbara wasn't jealous of the time she spent with her dog. After Evelyn's death, she'd spent most of her time with Barbara, who'd helped her through her depression. Since she'd taken her life back into her own hands, however, they saw each other once or twice a week at most. Perhaps Barbara missed Joyce.

"Oh god, Joyce, get that filthy thing away from me," Barbara said, pointing at the crate Joyce was holding.

Or perhaps she's Cruella de Vil reincarnated, Joyce thought as she put the crate down and motioned her sister inside. "Sorry, I had to fetch it out of the basement because Dingo will need to sleep in it until he's fully recovered so he doesn't hurt himself. Can I get you something to drink?"

"Well, that's one good thing about this accident then. You won't have that beast and all of his germs in bed with you for a while." Barbara followed Joyce to the kitchen and placed her purse on the beige granite countertop. "I'll have a glass of white wine if you have any," she said before she took her usual seat on the light tan leather of one of the three stools that lined up the breakfast bar.

Joyce flinched at Barbara's mention of Dingo's germs but didn't protest. She also chose to ignore her suggestion that she might not have white wine despite the fact that Barbara rarely came to her home without asking for white wine and having as much as she wanted served to her each and every time. "Chardonnay okay?" she asked, not waiting for an answer before opening the door of the dark oak cabinet where she kept her wineglasses.

"Perfect."

Joyce took the bottle out of the stainless steel built-in wine cooler and opened it in silence before she poured two glasses. Unlike her sister she didn't drink wine like water, but she figured she'd particularly enjoy it after the day she'd had.

"Where is the beast now?" Barbara asked after she took her first sip of wine.

"Sleeping in the living room. The painkillers knocked him out."

"Good. So you're free to come have dinner at home with me. Heather's going to bring her latest conquest and I could use your support." Barbara rolled her eyes and Joyce had to laugh. Her sister's incisive humor always made her laugh when it wasn't directed at Dingo. Barbara giggled in her turn and her features relaxed. This was the Barbara she enjoyed spending time with.

"I'm serious, Joyce. I can't get through another dinner with one of Heather's wandering souls without your support. Why can't she find a woman who knows what she wants out of life? This crap was cute when she was twenty, but she's going on thirty now. You and Evelyn were already an old couple at that age, for god's sake."

"Not all lesbians are the same, Barbara. How many times do I have to tell you?" Joyce declared as she kept laughing. She'd always been proud of the way Barbara had accepted and supported her daughter when she'd come out of the closet in her late teens, but she wished she could find a way to keep her from comparing the young woman to her older lesbian aunt, who'd been in a serious and successful long-term relationship for most of her life. It wasn't fair to Heather.

That said she had to agree with Barbara on the questionable characters of the women Heather chose to date. They all seemed to be spineless, ghostly little creatures molding themselves to Heather's personality until Heather got tired of them, which was usually within two or three months. They'd had big hopes for Sandra, who'd lasted six months, but Sandra's ghost eventually had vanished like all the others. Joyce hoped Heather would fall for a different type of woman someday. A woman with drive who would have a life and a personality of her own and who would challenge Heather instead of becoming her puppet. Amanda Carter's pretty freckled face and brandy-brown eyes popped into Joyce's mind and she smiled to herself. *That would never work. No way in hell.*

"So you'll come? Please say yes."

Joyce's mind went back to Dingo and she shook her head. "I can't, Barb. I'm sorry. I have to keep an eye on Dingo and give him his painkillers a little later. Plus I'm dead tired. It's been quite a day."

Joyce expected Barbara to insist, but instead she felt her sister's hand tapping her own and she heard resignation in her tone when she spoke, "I figured you'd say that, but it was worth a try. Wish me luck, then, Baby Sis. I'm off to try to make conversation with another empty, drifting mind."

Joyce chuckled. "Good luck. Try not to grill her on politics and current events."

Joyce watched Barbara empty her glass of wine and grab her purse before she turned to Joyce with a Machiavellian smile. "Why not, dear? It's so much fun watching them shrivel in their ignorance like tiny, brainless raisins." She winked before she started walking to the front door.

"You're evil," Joyce declared as she followed her.

"I know, dear."

After Barbara left, she went to the living room to check on Dingo. He was sitting in his bed, looking out the patio door that led to the backyard. The painkillers were beginning to lose their hold on him, but he still looked half asleep as he contemplated the yard, his playing turf, with heavy eyelids. The wrinkles on his forehead made him look almost as pitiful as the basset hound she'd focused on while sitting in the waiting room of the clinic. She studied the way the light of the low evening sun hit his red fur and his dark eyes, then turned quietly to get her painting supplies.

She'd started painting about six months ago. Dingo had been her inspiration then, just like today. The contrast of his fur with the grass he was running in had reminded Joyce she'd liked to paint before college and adult life had left her with no time for her watercolors. She'd purchased the supplies she needed and started to paint Dingo. Dingo playing. Dingo sleeping. Dingo running. Then other animals: squirrels, birds, other dogs she'd met in the park. She even had a painting of Slipper, the Bernese mountain dog, somewhere. She finished each watercolor with splatters. It added a level of risk to her art that she enjoyed. She never knew where the splashes of color would fall, if they would enhance her painting or ruin it. It added a playful element to her art, and that's what she wanted. She didn't dream of becoming a serious artist. She was simply having fun. Painting relaxed her and stimulated her all at once, and it was a pleasure she was certain she couldn't live without anymore.

Joyce started painting Dingo, including the black bandage and red water hydrant. This painting would be the ultimate memento of this crazy day. It would mark not only his injury, but the beginning of his recovery and the day they met the intriguing Doctor Amanda Carter. The Seeker. Joyce couldn't help feeling this eventful seventh of July was the beginning of yet another new chapter in her life, and any new chapter deserved a painting.

CHAPTER SIX

Amanda wished she'd kept her mouth shut. But no, she had to tell Joyce it was her birthday, didn't she? If she hadn't said anything she'd be on her way home by now. Instead she was standing uncomfortably around a store-bought cake with the entire staff. First there was Isabelle, who seemed all too proud of herself. Next to her were Chloe and Matt, the two other vet techs who worked at the clinic, and Jacqueline, their office manager. Doug stood by Amanda and appeared as embarrassed by the setting as she was.

Fortunately they didn't sing "Happy Birthday." They simply said the words out loud and even that brief announcement was out of synch and cacophonic. Amanda thanked them and then hurried to cut the cake and place each generous piece on a small paper plate which she handed to the members of the staff with a napkin and a plastic fork. The three vet techs and Jacqueline went to eat their cake at one end of the minuscule break room while Amanda and Doug stayed alone at the other end.

Doug meticulously removed the white frosting from the chocolate cake before he started eating. "Not a fan of frosting?" she asked with a smile as she took a bite of her own piece of cake. It was a little dry but not too bad for something bought from a grocery store at the last minute. Isabelle was right to be proud.

"Nah, it's way too sweet." She wasn't surprised by his answer. She'd noticed he rarely ate sweets. She was certain it was not a question of weight though. He was about six feet tall and skinny as a thermometer. With round glasses and thinning brown hair, at first glance he looked like the epitome of the nerd. But he also had striking aquamarine blue eyes that seemed to make their female vet techs weak at the knees, judging by a conversation she'd caught between Isabelle and Chloe. Of course he was clueless about his charms and the effect he had on their employees.

"You should have told me your birthday was coming up, Amanda. I could have gotten you a gift. Or at least a card." Doug seemed genuinely saddened by Amanda's lack of disclosure. His distress perplexed her. She swallowed her bite of cake with a hint of guilt.

"I'm sorry. I don't usually share this kind of information with people I work with. I didn't mean to mention it at all actually. It just came out of my mouth."

Doug had picked at his piece of cake with his fork while Amanda spoke and when she finished he set the plate and fork on the table and cleared his throat before he looked her straight in the eye. "My birthday is in October. October eleventh, to be exact." He scratched at his neck nervously and blinked several times, clearly uncomfortable with their conversation, yet determined to continue.

"Okay. I'll put it on my calendar," she said hesitantly, unsure if it was the right thing to say. She didn't understand what had gotten into him.

"Good. I think we should know these things about each other. We're not only coworkers, after all. We're partners. I don't even know how old you are."

"Right. I'm thirty-two."

"Good. I'm forty-three." Amanda nodded and a silence followed during which they stared at each other until he spoke again. "Susan and I would like to have you over for dinner soon."

"Susan?" Amanda was certain Doug was going somewhere with this strange exchange, but she couldn't figure out where yet. His transitions—or lack thereof—were unsettling to say the least.

"My wife. We'd like you to come to our house for dinner."

"Oh. Sure, that would be lovely." She watched as a timid smile took shape on his lips and guessed she'd given the right answer.

"Great. I'll let you know when."

"Okay." Doug granted her a final nod of acknowledgment and left the break room. She shook her head. It might be easy and natural to work with someone who was as socially challenged as she was, but having a conversation with that same person was a completely different thing. She glanced at the staff at the other end of the break room. They were engrossed in their own, much less awkward conversation. She headed for the door, deciding that the timing was perfect to make her escape unnoticed.

Amanda pondered how strange and unexpected this birthday had been as she walked the three miles from the clinic to her condo on Franklin Street. She made the trek almost every day, with the exception of days when she was running late or the weather was bad. Walking got her head ready for work in the morning and cleared it of work-related issues at night. Fresh air was magical like that.

Why was Doug suddenly interested in getting to know her on a more personal level? Was his wife responsible for his efforts? Or was he not quite as socially inept as she was after all? Perhaps partners in a business should know things like their respective birthdays or the name of their partner's wife. Perhaps that kind of stuff was more important to him than she'd thought. It scared her to some extent, but at the same time she figured that if she absolutely had to make friends with someone, he was not a bad choice.

As she left the street to cut through Broadway Park she replaced thoughts of Doug with ones about Joyce Allen, free now to let the sophisticated beauty occupy her mind without any restraint.

She gave a wry grin. In her musings, it was so easy, so natural. They spoke of numerology and cared for Dingo as if they'd known each other all their lives. Getting to that point in real life was another story. She had no idea how to approach any woman, let alone a woman as sophisticated as Joyce. Her heart raced with anxiety at the mere thought of talking to her outside of an exam room.

She took a deep breath as she entered a red brick building and climbed up the stairs to the second floor to her two-bedroom condo. She needed to focus on something else. Entering the small modern foyer, she contemplated the boxes filling half of the living room. She decided now was as good a time as any to finish unpacking, to really settle in. She still had a million questions about her future, but one thing had become clear today. She was in Bangor to stay.

CHAPTER SEVEN

Joyce carried Dingo into the clinic and informed the nice woman sitting at the reception desk of their arrival. She sat in the waiting room, placed her purse on the chair beside her, and installed Dingo comfortably on her lap. Glancing at the poster with the basset hound with a broken leg, she yawned. "I bet he lets his mommy sleep," she told the basenji, who looked back at her with his usual pitiful frown. "Those forehead wrinkles don't work on me anymore, little brat. Try again after I've had some sleep." Dingo sighed and closed his eyes.

Amanda had given them her first morning appointment and the waiting room was empty. Joyce was grateful. She felt like a truck had rolled over her a few times, forward and backward. As she waited patiently with Dingo she checked the position of the scarf around her neck. She'd chosen a silk one in tones of reds, purples, and blues that she wore with a deep red shell top. She also was wearing more makeup than usual, hoping to hide the paleness of her face and the bags under her eyes caused by the lack of sleep.

The past two weeks had been challenging. No, they'd been hell. Dingo's late-night yodels before his injury had always been annoying, but they eventually stopped and they both went to sleep together. This was different. He didn't understand why he couldn't sleep in bed with her anymore and made the most heartrending sounds the whole time he was in his crate. Screeching yodels that could only be interpreted as crying kept Joyce up all night, leaving her to grab a few minutes of sleep here and there while he slept on his dog bed during the day. All day long. Snoring away.

"Doctor Carter is ready for you, Ms. Allen."

Joyce's eyes popped open at the sound of Isabelle's voice. When had she closed them? And for how long? She feared she'd been sleeping.

"Oh, hi. Okay, yes. Lead on." She pushed the strap of her purse up to her shoulder, gathered Dingo into her arms, and followed Isabelle to the exam room they'd been in two weeks ago. She just had time to place Dingo on the exam table before Amanda arrived. She smiled at the pretty veterinarian, realizing as she did so that the way her facial muscles tensed up at the simple act meant she probably hadn't smiled much in the past several days. "Good morning, Amanda."

"Good morning," Amanda answered with a bright smile and a slight blush on her cheeks. She was so lovely, Joyce thought. "So, tell me about the past two weeks," she added as she brought her attention to Dingo and started petting him softly.

"Pure hell," Joyce said honestly, her candor surprising herself as much as Amanda, who giggled nervously. "He won't let me sleep," she explained. "Do I really need to keep him in his crate?"

"I'm afraid so," Amanda said with compassion. She placed her hand on Joyce's as she'd done during their first visit and the touch had the same calming effect on her it had had that first time. Joyce knew she would believe whatever she'd say next. "But you have to sleep too, Joyce."

Joyce snorted a laugh. "I know, but Dingo in crate and Joyce getting some sleep are not compatible, unfortunately. Do you have sleeping pills you can prescribe?"

"For Dingo?"

"For me! For both of us! Whatever will work. I need to sleep. I really, really need to sleep." She punctuated her declaration with exaggerated, desperate gestures before she ended with a heartfelt, "Please." If they could see her, she knew that Barbara and Evelyn would tell her she was acting like a drama queen. She half expected Amanda to do the same. Instead, the young doctor took Joyce's hand between hers and smiled with empathy.

"I can prescribe something for Dingo if we have to, but I'd like to try something else first. Something you might not like."

"What? I'll do anything. Tell me what to do and I'll do it, I promise." Amanda chuckled at her desperate plea and squeezed her hand.

"Well, let me ask you something first. When Dingo cries at night, what do you do?"

"I try to comfort him, I yell at him to be quiet. Nothing works though. He keeps crying."

"So, Dingo cries and Dingo gets attention. Am I correct?"

"Yes," Joyce admitted shamefully, understanding what she'd been doing wrong. After all the reading she'd done on dog training it took Amanda to make her realize she'd been doing exactly the one thing she shouldn't have done: giving Dingo attention when he was asking for it. "I wasn't supposed to do that, was I?"

Amanda shook her head slowly, still smiling, and Joyce wondered how the woman was capable of showing compassion even as she was reprimanding her.

"Let's do this. Before we give Dingo sleeping pills, why don't you try ignoring him tonight? If it gets too difficult, move his crate to another room in the house, as far from your bedroom as possible. I promise you he will stop crying. It might take a while, but he will. Okay?"

"Okay, that makes sense." With new hopes that she might get some sleep tonight at last, Joyce turned her attention to Dingo and his bandage. After all, his injured leg was the reason why they were in an exam room with Amanda this morning. They weren't here for her to get therapy, although Amanda seemed awfully talented at making her feel better. She felt safe and at peace in her presence. A few minutes with the young redhead brought her even more serenity than an hour of yoga. And she loved yoga.

"Perfect," Amanda concluded as she released Joyce's hand. Joyce left her warm hand on the table, hoping for her touch to return. But Amanda was all business. "Besides the lack of sleep, how are things going with Dingo? Has he been eating and drinking normally?"

"Yes."

"Urinating normally as well?"

"Yes."

"Any soft stools?"

"No, that's normal too."

"Great. So we'll change that bandage and you'll be on your way."

"Sounds like a plan," Joyce said although she was in no hurry to leave Amanda.

She took a step back and watched quietly as Amanda and Isabelle proceeded to remove Dingo's bandage. Dingo fought minimally when the two women forced him on his side, but he lay still and obediently as they started working on the bandage. It didn't take long before a rancid smell started emanating from the bandage. Joyce moved closer to the table to see what might be causing that awful odor. She didn't know how to describe it. What came to mind was death. Putrid, rotting death. The aroma quickly filled the small room. Joyce placed a hand over her nose as she examined Dingo's leg, spotting sores in a few places.

"Oh my god. Is it infected? Is he going to lose his leg?"

Amanda had stopped smiling, but her tone remained calm. "No. He's not going to lose his leg. He does have a few sores I don't like, but we'll take care of them. It happens a lot. That's why we want to change the bandage often. What we'll do is give him antibiotics to make sure the sores don't get infected." She turned to Joyce and smiled and Joyce was almost reassured.

"But what about this smell?"

"It's pretty bad, isn't it?" Amanda admitted with a chuckle. "It's bacteria. Stuck under that bandage it gets vile. That's another reason why we need to change Dingo's bandage often. Don't worry. We'll clean Dingo's leg, let it dry, put antibiotic cream on his sores, give him a brand-new bandage, and send you home with more antibiotics to give him orally every day. All of this is perfectly normal, but it will take a little longer than expected this morning. Do you have errands to run or would you like to…"

"I'll wait," Joyce interrupted.

"I knew it," Amanda said with another, wider smile. "I'll take him in the back and we'll call you when he's ready, okay?"

"Okay." Joyce watched Amanda leave with Dingo before she let Isabelle escort her to the waiting room.

She sat on her usual chair and breathed deeply in and out as she focused on the basset hound facing her. "It will be all right," she said to the poster, taking advantage of a still empty waiting room. And she really trusted her words. Unbelievably, she'd gone in a few minutes from a grumpy sleep-deprived old woman to the hopeful, relaxed woman she much preferred to be. Just a few minutes in Doctor Amanda Carter's exam room. In her presence. There was definitely something special about that young woman. Something that brought out the best in her.

Joyce didn't quite understand why or how, but her instinct told her Amanda Carter had an important part to play in her life, perhaps in helping her let her true self shine. Her instinct also told her that part was too important to be limited to an exam room or even to this veterinary clinic. Joyce needed to find a way to spend time with Amanda outside of this place. She couldn't get to know her better with the observant eyes of the vet tech or a few minutes at a time while she changed Dingo's bandage. No, they needed more time. To talk. She wanted to know what Amanda the Seeker was looking for exactly. She wanted to know her philosophy of life, what mattered to her, what made her smile other than a neurotic client who needed to sleep.

But how? What would make a beautiful young woman like Amanda want to spend time with an older woman like herself?

She couldn't simply invite her for coffee. That would probably scare her.

Joyce laughed to herself. She'd never been shy before. Then again, she'd never met someone she so desperately wanted to get to know better. She was the one being constantly invited to mundane events. Invitations she often refused, preferring to go spend some time at the museum or even attend a concert by herself.

She focused on the poster across from her, determined to come up with a brilliant idea before Dingo was ready to leave the doctor's care today. She wouldn't leave the clinic until she'd made plans with Amanda. Who cared about their age difference? She wasn't going to ask the veterinarian on a date after all. She would simply propose an activity they could enjoy together. She would offer her friendship. Amanda wouldn't be able to say no to her. Very few people could say no to Joyce when she really wanted something. And right now, she really wanted Amanda in her life.

CHAPTER EIGHT

When Amanda came back to the exam room with Dingo and his freshly wrapped leg, she saw an expression on Joyce's face that she didn't recognize. Her smile and her almond-shaped anthracite eyes had in them something mischievous and inquisitive she hadn't seen before. She hadn't seen many of Joyce's expressions yet, of course, and she wanted to know all of them, but she found this particular one unsettling. She'd been proud of herself for keeping her nerves under control earlier, but she wasn't certain she could keep her composure under this new, almost intrusive stare. The more she tried to remain aloof, the more her mind flashed back to the delicate hand she'd been holding to reassure Joyce, to the softness of her skin. She flushed, convinced that Joyce could read every thought she was having.

She nervously pushed her glasses up the bridge of her nose with her index finger. "So Dingo is all set. He was a very good boy during the entire process. Some dogs need to be sedated every time we change their bandage, but fortunately it won't be the case with him," she said quickly, trying to keep her mind on business.

"Great. That's good to know. Have you treated a lot of dogs with broken legs around here?"

"Not around here. I've only been here for two months. But I did treat several broken legs when I worked in Portland."

"Two months? So you're new in town then?"

"Yes." Amanda was yet again surprised at how easy it was to divulge information to Joyce. While the tiniest of revelations was torture with anyone else, it seemed natural with her. And the way Joyce's smile widened made it seem like she was especially satisfied with this specific revelation. If she had a minute alone with her, the privacy might help Joyce come forward with the reason why the fact that Amanda was new to Bangor made her so happy.

"Isabelle, would you go get Dingo's antibiotics ready while I explain to Ms. Allen how to give them to him?"

"Of course," Isabelle agreed before exiting the room.

"Have you ever given Dingo medicine orally using a syringe or a dropper?"

"Yes. I need to empty the contents of the syringe right here, correct?" Joyce said as she touched the side of Dingo's mouth toward the back teeth.

"That's right. The antibiotics we're giving you come with a dropper so you'll be all set," Amanda said. She focused on Dingo's mouth as she felt Joyce observe her.

"So what brought you to Bangor? Do you have family here? Friends?"

"No. Doctor Perry offered me partnership in his clinic so I moved here."

"Just like that, huh?" Joyce said playfully.

"Just like that. It was a great career move and I love it here. I can get lost in nature," Amanda confirmed before she found the courage to meet Joyce's gaze.

"Well, congratulations on the partnership. Dingo and I sure think Doctor Perry chose wisely. You've been amazing. With both of us." Joyce winked at her and she felt her cheeks warm up to the point of discomfort.

"Thank you," she managed to answer although her voice sounded like a whisper to her own ears.

"I mean it. In fact, I'd like to do something special to thank you."

Amanda swallowed painfully. "It's not necessary. I'm only doing my job."

"I know. But you're doing it remarkably well and I would love to do something to thank you. Please let me."

Joyce placed a hand on Amanda's shoulder, making her overwhelmingly aware of the three or four inches Joyce had over her own five feet five. She was also powerfully aware of their proximity. A part of her wanted to run, but a less familiar part of her took over as she answered, "Okay. What did you have in mind?"

"Well, next weekend is the opening of the Bangor State Fair. Have you heard about it?"

"I've seen signs at the grocery store," Amanda admitted, panicking at the thought of the crowd an event such as this one might attract.

"I thought it might be fun. What do you think?"

"I don't know," Amanda replied, on the verge of a full-blown panic attack. Joyce gently squeezed her shoulder, forcing her to lock eyes with her.

"I'd love to take you to the fair. Please let me."

Amanda couldn't help but acquiesce.

"Okay. I'll go," she agreed with a smile she hoped didn't betray any of the anxiety she was feeling.

When Isabelle came back with Dingo's antibiotics, Joyce dropped the hand that had been resting on Amanda's shoulder. Amanda's anxiety instantly skyrocketed. It was as if Joyce's hand, somehow, had been containing it and now that it was gone it was going through the roof. Amanda wanted to renege, to say she couldn't go to the fair after all. But it was too late. Isabelle was back in the room and saying something now would be... awkward.

Joyce picked up Dingo and headed toward the door. "Thank you, Amanda. I'll call you later this week. To schedule Dingo's next appointment," she added with a mischievous wink.

* * *

Later that evening Amanda sat on her balcony looking over the Kenduskeag Stream, fiddling with her cell phone and watching people walk and bike the trail that started almost right next to her building. It was one of the main reasons she'd chosen her condo, that and the proximity of the University of Maine Museum of Art and several restaurants and cafés she rarely frequented but made her neighborhood pleasant nonetheless.

She'd decided to call and cancel the trip to the fair, but she couldn't muster up the courage to dial the number she'd gotten from Dingo's file. As much as she wanted to spend time with Joyce, Amanda didn't think she could face the crowd there.

She'd avoided crowds for as long as she could remember. They made her so anxious she'd concluded she suffered from mild agoraphobia. Since she was capable of confronting her fear when she was obligated to, like when she had to go to professional conventions, she'd never sought treatment for her condition. Even as a kid, however, she'd always hated fairs. Fortunately, her mother hadn't found the time or money to take her often. She recalled two or three times, all nightmares. She might have enjoyed the fair if she could have stayed around the animals, but her mother and her boyfriend *du jour* always insisted on playing games instead or taking rides she had no inclination for whatsoever.

She couldn't go to the fair with Joyce. What if she had a panic attack in her company? What kind of impression would that give her? She couldn't risk it.

Amanda dialed the first five digits of Joyce's phone number with temporarily found bravery before she set the phone down on the table. Then again, what if Joyce took her cancellation of their plans as definite disinterest and didn't ask her to do anything else? Was that a risk she was willing to take? Probably not. Absolutely not.

She sighed and emptied her glass of iced tea in one large gulp. *All right, big baby. If you can find the guts to go to a convention with a bunch of boring veterinarians, you can find the guts to go to the fair with the most fascinating woman you've ever met. That's an order, Carter.*

CHAPTER NINE

The following Saturday Joyce woke up late—hallelujah—
and spent time in the yard with Dingo. She couldn't let him
exercise as much as he wanted to, but she was relieved that he
could put more weight on his bandaged leg. She couldn't help
but smile as she ate her toast and drank her coffee. It wasn't only
because of Dingo. Today was the day she was taking Amanda
to the fair. She was both excited and nervous at the thought of
spending time with the young woman outside of the veterinary
clinic. She couldn't remember the last time she'd looked forward
to doing something or going somewhere with another person.
Since Evelyn's death she'd taken the most pleasure in activities
she could plan and do by herself. This enthusiasm for going to
the fair with Amanda was new and welcome. Even the sun was
back after a few days of rain, apparently wanting to take part in
this unfamiliar ferment.

After she finished her breakfast Joyce took Dingo back
inside where he lay on his dog bed while she showered and got
dressed. She then installed Dingo in his crate with one of his

favorite toys, a rubber ball that she filled with treats. It would keep him busy for hours. She didn't like leaving him in his crate every time she went out, but she understood it was the best way to keep him safe. Besides, three nights of ignoring his whining had been enough to cure him of his separation anxiety and he seemed to find his crate a lot more pleasurable now. For the past few nights, he'd whimpered for barely a minute or two before falling asleep, which allowed her to sleep soundly as well. It was a small miracle she was very grateful for. She couldn't wait to thank Amanda in person for her help. She was going to have to, unfortunately. She was almost ready to leave when Barbara arrived unannounced with a bottle of sparkling wine.

"Do you have orange juice? It's time for mimosas."

"Of course I have orange juice, Barb, but are we celebrating something? It's kind of early to start drinking," Joyce answered as she closed the door behind her sister and followed her into the kitchen. It was a few minutes past noon and Joyce was due to pick up Amanda in an hour to go to the state fair. She'd planned on going to return books at the library beforehand but that could wait, she decided as she grabbed two champagne flutes out of the cupboard.

"That's why I thought of mimosas, dear sister. Mimosas were invented to give women an excuse to drink as early as they want. And this woman wants a drink," Barbara concluded as she raised a hand over her head and pointed to herself with her index finger.

"If you say so," Joyce said with a chuckle. She reached for the orange juice in the fridge and poured some in the champagne flutes while Barbara opened the sparkling wine. "So, not exactly celebrating, then?"

"That's too much juice in my glass, Joy," Barbara said with a wink before she continued. "We could celebrate the fact that Heather dumped Sloane last night if you want."

Joyce carefully transferred some orange juice from one glass to the other, thinking she'd be happy to drink more juice than wine. "Sloane?"

"Sloane, yes. The specter my daughter has been dating for a month." Barbara filled the rest of their glasses with wine. "But that's right. You didn't get to meet her, did you?"

"No, I didn't. I haven't seen Heather for a while, actually. What happened?"

"Oh, same old story. Heather got tired of her. She says Sloane got too possessive and didn't challenge her enough. Blah, blah, blah, same crap, different girl."

"That's too bad," Joyce offered, relieved that she didn't have time to meet this young woman. Not that she would have let herself get attached. She'd learned a long time ago that the women in Heather's life were like clouds passing over their heads. "And what did you tell Heather?"

"Same thing I always tell her. You can't expect an empty brain to challenge you, child." Barbara handed a glass to Joyce and held her own in front of her to propose a toast. "To Sloane. May her broken heart heal quickly and may her brain keep wandering aimlessly!"

"To Sloane," Joyce said as they solemnly clanked their glasses together before she burst out laughing. She didn't want to make fun of the poor girl she didn't even know, but she couldn't resist her sister's humor.

"Did you ever think maybe she picks women who don't challenge her because she's scared she'll end up with someone like you?" Joyce was shocked at her own question. It was one that had been burning her lips for years, but she'd never dared to let it out before. She expected Barbara to protest but instead her sister focused on the orange liquid in her glass. The silence was so uncomfortable she felt compelled to explain, "I mean, you have to admit you're very opinionated. Your opinions have a big influence on Heather even though they often clash with her own ideas. Maybe she doesn't want more ideas to fight against in her life. Maybe. That's just a thought I had."

Barbara finally met Joyce's gaze again and huffed. "If that's the case, she needs to get over it. She's old enough to stand up for herself, after all. I stood up to our mother, didn't I?" Joyce nodded in agreement, biting her tongue to make sure she wouldn't comment about the spineless man Barbara had chosen for a husband. The more she thought about it, the more she was convinced Heather was simply following in her mother's footsteps.

They heard a yodel coming from upstairs. Joyce remembered Dingo was in his crate and cringed. *Poor little brat.* Barbara grimaced as she did every time she heard Dingo yodel.

"Oh my god. That sound's unbearable. I don't know how you do it. Where's the little sack of germs anyway?"

"He's in his crate in my bedroom upstairs. I was about to leave the house when you arrived."

"And where were you going dressed like that?" Barbara asked as she gave Joyce the familiar, judgmental once-over.

Joyce looked down at her clean dark blue jeans and sleeveless white blouse. She fixed the turquoise silk scarf around her neck and the understated silver bracelet on her wrist. She was satisfied with her look. It was on the casual side, perhaps, but it wasn't as if she was wearing sweats. Her attire might have contrasted with Barbara's white designer suit and array of jewelry, but the question Joyce didn't dare to ask was where her sister was going that justified wearing a two-thousand-dollar suit anyway. "I'm going to the fair, Barb. What else am I supposed to wear?" she answered before she sighed with annoyance.

"The fair?" Barbara raised an eyebrow and laughed condescendingly. "Oh Baby Sis, aren't we a little old for that? I hope you weren't expecting me to go with you because…"

"I wasn't," Joyce interrupted with an abrupt, defensive tone. "If you must know everything I'm going with a new friend: Dingo's vet. And in case you haven't noticed, I'm making an effort to do all kinds of things these days. Just because you don't like something or Evelyn wouldn't have liked it doesn't mean I have to dislike it too."

"You're going to the fair with Doctor Perry?" Joyce was disheartened by her sister's choice to completely ignore her call for independence, yet couldn't help but join her in laughter when she stopped to imagine herself going to the fair with Doctor Perry. He was a nice guy, but she'd never been able to get more than two words out of him during her first visits at the clinic with Dingo. He was beyond awkward. She and Barbara had often discussed Doctor Perry's lack of social skills since they'd sat together with him on a charity committee a few years ago.

"No, not Doctor Perry. I'm going with Dingo's new vet, Amanda Carter," she said as she wiped a tear of laughter at the corner of her eye.

"Oh, a female vet. And so the plot thickens," Barbara said with a teasing wink. "Now I understand why you're willing to go to the stinky fair. Trying to impress a woman, huh? It's about time, if you ask me. But now obviously you have to tell me everything you know about this Amanda Carter. Spill it out." Barbara emptied her glass and refilled it with sparkling wine, not bothering with the orange juice and the mimosa excuse this time.

"It's not like that, silly. She's way too young for one thing. I'm simply grateful for what she's done for me and Dingo and I wanted to do something nice to thank her. She's new in town and doesn't know anyone so I'm hoping we can become friends."

"Friends? You're really expecting me to buy that? You can tell me you know. Evelyn was a wonderful woman and we were close, but she wouldn't want you to be alone for the rest of your lesbian life. And neither do I."

Joyce was moved by Barbara's declaration. She'd thought Barbara would be opposed to her dating anyone else and she was relieved to know that wouldn't be the case. Dating Amanda, however, was not her intention. "I swear, Barb," Joyce insisted as she felt her face heat up and she loosened the scarf around her neck. "She's at least twenty years younger than I am, for god's sake. I just want to offer my friendship. She's a fascinating person and I want to get to know her better, but as a friend."

"Okay, I believe you. If she's as young as you say she is it wouldn't be appropriate for you to want more anyway. Friendship is already a little weird if you ask me."

"Well, I'm not asking you."

"Is she gay?"

"I don't know," Joyce said as she was forced to admit to herself that although her intuition told her Amanda was a lesbian, she truly didn't know for sure.

"Well, try to find out, will you? If she is we could try to match her with Heather. She's about her age, isn't she?"

"She is," Joyce confirmed regretfully. The thought of Amanda with Heather made her stomach tighten for some reason. Heather was her niece, but she was also a heartbreaker. The last thing she wanted was to cause Amanda any pain.

"Great. Find out if she's gay then. Can you imagine? A veterinarian would be such a nice change from all of Heather's past girlfriends. I'm sure if she met someone like that she'd finally settle in. And I'd finally stop worrying so much about her." Barbara's plea touched Joyce. She wasn't convinced Amanda and Heather would make such a good match but there was no point in voicing her opinion yet.

"Okay, I'll try to find out. But I'm warning you, it won't be easy. Amanda is reserved. Not exactly an open book, if you know what I mean."

"I don't doubt it, but I also know how good you are at extracting information when you really want to." Barbara emptied her glass again and grabbed her purse from the counter.

"I'll try, that's all I can promise." Joyce followed her sister to the front door.

"And that's all I want. Now let me get out of your hair so you can get to your mission." They shared air kisses and she opened the door for Barbara, who started walking to her Mercedes and added without turning around, "Have fun with the smelly cows and have a greasy hot dog for me!"

CHAPTER TEN

Joyce stopped her Subaru Forester in front of Amanda's building on Franklin Street. She looked at her surroundings with nostalgia. She'd smiled to herself when Amanda had given her the address earlier that week. Franklin Street represented so much for her. She didn't have time to get lost in her memories, however, as Amanda climbed in the passenger seat and greeted her timidly. "Hi. Have you been waiting for long?"

"I just got here actually. Hello," Joyce replied as she studied Amanda for a few seconds. She wore jeans and a light gray T-shirt with a darker gray, long, loose-knit sweater over it. It was the first time Joyce had seen her wearing anything other than scrubs and a lab coat, and she thought that although the relaxed layered look suited her, it made her look even younger. If it wasn't for her dark-framed glasses and familiar ponytail, Joyce might not even have recognized her. "I love this neighborhood. You know I worked across the street from your building for nearly thirty years?"

"At the bank?"

"Mhm. I was in marketing. That's where the corporate offices are located," she said as she pointed to the old building. "I haven't been back to Franklin Street since I retired over a year ago."

"Get out, you're retired? You don't look old enough to be retired."

"Well, I'm a young retiree," Joyce offered with a grin, trying to make Amanda relax a little. She seemed extremely nervous, constantly fidgeting with the strap of her messenger bag and unable to hold Joyce's gaze.

"I hope I didn't force you to face bad memories. I could have met you somewhere else, you know."

"Don't be silly," Joyce protested as she placed a hand on Amanda's arm, successfully making her meet her gaze at last. "I have fond memories of this place, actually. I do come to the neighborhood often, but I tend to stick to Central Street. I go to the museum or to the Bagel Café? Have you ever been?"

"A few times. To both places."

"A New Yorker would never call what they make at the Café a real bagel, but they do make a delicious breakfast. Maybe we could go some time."

"Maybe."

"You've chosen a lovely neighborhood. You must be happy here."

"I can't complain. But my favorite part is the walking and biking trail by the water."

"I see," Joyce said with a smile.

"Maybe we can go there some time too. I mean, maybe. If you want to." Amanda lowered her eyes to her messenger bag again and a dark blush covered her cheeks.

Joyce, whose hand was still resting on Amanda's arm, squeezed gently to reassure her companion. "I'd love to," she said sincerely. A walk with Amanda sounded lovely. "But today let's start with the state fair. Are you ready? You do know it's close to eighty degrees out there, right?" she asked as she patted the thick sleeve covering Amanda's arm.

Amanda laughed. "I know, but I'm often cold when other people are hot. So layers are a smart choice more than a fashion statement."

"Okay then, let's go." Joyce couldn't help but notice Amanda became even more nervous as she put both her hands back on the steering wheel and drove away from Franklin Street. The young woman clutched her messenger bag and clenched her teeth. Joyce hoped she wouldn't be in that state of mind all afternoon. She wanted to share a nice moment with Amanda, not torture her.

Unfortunately Amanda's nervousness seemed to reach new heights as they entered the state fair grounds and Joyce prepared to park. Her breathing became loud and fast and when Joyce glanced at her she saw that her eyes were shut tight. Joyce parked the car and stopped the engine before she turned to Amanda and placed her hand on a fist that she'd tightened around the strap of her messenger bag. "Are you okay? What's happening? Please tell me how I can help."

As soon as Joyce touched her Amanda started taking deeper breaths. Soon she felt the hand she was covering relax. As Amanda released her grip on the leather strap, she dared to caress Amanda's hand with her palm. She waited for Amanda to open her eyes and face her.

"I'm better now. I'm sorry. I don't do well with crowds and going to the fair is making me very anxious. I should have told you before we left, but I thought I had it under control."

"Oh my god, my poor child. Do you want to do something else instead? I don't want to force you out of your comfort zone. I simply want to spend a little time with you."

Amanda's smile softened her features and made her look calmer. Joyce hoped it wasn't an illusion. She felt such guilt for putting her through this misery. "That's what I want too. I'm okay now. We can go."

"Are you sure?" Joyce asked as she squeezed her hand.

"I'm sure. Just…" Amanda looked down again. Joyce placed her finger under the young woman's chin, tenderly moving her face back up toward her and looking into her eyes.

"Just what? Say it."

"Just don't leave me alone, okay?"

"Of course not," Joyce said with a smile, sighing with relief at the easy request. "I've got you, okay?" Amanda nodded and they got out of the car.

An hour later as they walked through the agricultural exhibits, stopping to pet animals here and there, Amanda had almost forgotten how she'd made a fool of herself in the car. Despite the rough beginning of their adventure at the fair, the day was turning out to be quite fun. She was relieved when Joyce confessed she wasn't a fan of scary rides and would be happier hanging out around animals. She'd probably guessed being around horses, cows, and other farm animals would make her feel more comfortable with the crowd. She was grateful for her sensitivity.

Amanda was impressed with her overall intuition as well. Every time she'd begun to feel anxious in the crowd surrounding them she'd felt Joyce's hand on her arm, shoulder, or back, and the contact always had a calming effect on her anxiety. Her touch caused other pleasant reactions in Amanda's body too, but she was choosing to ignore those for now, trying to avoid more reasons to be anxious. Today was a lovely day with a lovely woman, nothing more.

Actually, Joyce was beyond lovely. Even wearing jeans and a simple white blouse, she remained the embodiment of elegance, yet she didn't look out of place in the middle of farm animals. She was the perfect mix of grace and simplicity which allowed Amanda to be at ease with her at the same time as she was attracted to her. It was a sensation she'd never known before, both intriguing and reassuring.

They walked by a food stand and Joyce's eyes lit up. "I'm dying for some cotton candy. That's the best part of the fair. Do you want some?"

"Sure," Amanda agreed, giggling at her excitement.

Joyce grabbed her hand and pulled her toward the stand. She ordered pink cotton candy for herself and turned to Amanda, "What color will you have?"

"I'm guessing she wants pink too. Like her mother," the man behind the counter declared with a playful wink. He wore a white hat over gray hair and smiled through a thick mustache. He seemed friendly and oblivious to the faux pas he'd just committed.

Amanda glanced at Joyce, whose expression had darkened. "I think I will have pink, like my *friend*," she said to the man, putting more emphasis on the second part of her declaration. The man nodded and got started on their cotton candy cones without another word.

They left the stand and walked side by side with their pink cotton candy cones. Amanda noticed theirs were larger than most and thought that the man's generosity was most likely his way to appease a guilty conscience. They walked quietly for a minute or two, focusing on the cotton candy, which they picked with their fingers before letting it melt in their mouths.

Joyce's silence worried Amanda. She seemed uncharacteristically contemplative. "I guess he's right. I could be your mother," she finally said. "How old are you? Twenty-five? Thirty?"

"Thirty-two."

"See? I would have given birth at twenty-four. That's perfectly plausible."

Amanda quickly calculated that made Joyce fifty-six years old. Her mother was forty the last time she'd seen her twelve years ago, but she'd already looked so much older than Joyce. The thought escaped her mind before she could stop it. "You look much younger than my mother, if that makes you feel better."

Joyce laughed. Her laughter was so free, loud, and unrestrained, so unlike her own low, hesitant, and contained laughter. "As a matter of fact, that does make me feel better, thank you."

"Great. Besides, I don't care about your age." Joyce smiled, but Amanda wasn't certain she believed her. "It's true. I feel comfortable with you. That's what matters."

"You might be right. I'm glad you feel comfortable with me, but I can't keep wondering how many of these people think like that cotton candy man. That I'm your mother. Or your aunt." Joyce picked more cotton candy with her fingers but hesitated before putting it in her mouth. "You know, my sister thinks being friends with a woman your age might not be appropriate. I'm sure Evelyn would agree with her."

"Evelyn?"

"My wife."

Amanda slowed down as she processed the information she'd been given. Joyce was married. She was unavailable. She really wanted nothing more than friendship and it would stay that way. Her heart broke instantly and she realized how much hope she'd put in this budding relationship. Too much hope.

"Your wife?" she simply said, unable to add more without betraying the extent of her dismay.

"Yes." Joyce stopped and looked at her. "Are you okay? Do you have a problem with me being a lesbian?"

"Oh no," Amanda quickly answered when she realized what Joyce might be thinking. "Of course not. I just didn't know you were married. I mean, you always come to the clinic alone with Dingo," she said, rambling on nervously until she felt the warmth of Joyce's hand on her arm.

"I *was* married to be exact. Evelyn died three years ago. I live alone with Dingo," Joyce explained. The instant relief overwhelmed Amanda. It wasn't normal or healthy for her to feel so happy about another woman's death, she chastised herself. "So you're okay with the fact that I'm gay, then? It's important for you to be if we're going to be friends."

"It's okay," Amanda confirmed. She hesitated before she continued, recognizing that she'd never told anyone about her own sexuality, mostly because she'd never needed to before. "I'm gay too, Joyce. So believe me, it's really okay."

"Good," Joyce said as she squeezed her arm. "That's really good." Amanda couldn't decipher what she saw in Joyce's smile and in her eyes in that moment. Satisfaction, perhaps. Relief, certainly. Joyce sure seemed very happy about Amanda's coming out, which told her she might have been right to put such high hopes in their new friendship after all. Joyce was single and she seemed suspiciously delighted to find out Amanda was gay. Those were good reasons to hope, weren't they?

They stayed to watch the horse-pulling contest but left before dinner. Joyce declared that although she wished they could stay it was probably a better idea to leave before the crowd started gathering for the country music concert that was scheduled that evening. Amanda was touched by her regard for her anxiety and agreed it would be safer to leave, yet she missed her the second she got out of the Subaru on Franklin Street. They hadn't made plans to meet again, but she found consolation in knowing they had an appointment to change Dingo's bandage the following Friday.

CHAPTER ELEVEN

Amanda sat on Doug's deck on Wednesday night, wondering what had gotten into her. He'd invited her over for dinner a couple of times since he'd threatened to do so on her birthday, but she'd managed to come up with excuses on both occasions. When he'd asked again on Monday, however, she'd accepted without hesitation. She didn't know if her change of heart was due to newly found courage after the overall success of her outing at the fair with Joyce or to the building desire to get this mandatory dinner over with, but here she was, eating veggie burgers with Doug and his family.

Fortunately, Doug's wife was a real word-mill. She never stopped talking and she didn't seem to care if anyone listened. It made it easy on Amanda; all she needed to do was nod or insert a simple "mhm" once in a while to keep the monologue going. She thought that quality of Susan's was most likely one of the reasons Doug had married her. She freed him from having to make conversation ever again in his whole life. *Smart man*, she mused.

But as she listened to Susan she had to admit her qualities weren't limited to her verbosity. She was also a very attractive petite woman with beautiful blue eyes and blond hair. Most importantly the abundant words coming out of her mouth betrayed nothing but kindness and generosity. She didn't talk to complain about people or judge them as it was often the case with women who talked that much. She talked about the poverty of the families she worked with as a social worker and the obstacles they lived through every single day. She talked about social issues and ways to overcome them. Her speech was engaging, admirable, and Amanda felt better about her own soul just listening to her.

As a result, an evening Amanda had been dreading was turning out to be surprisingly enjoyable. Which is why she seriously considered making her escape when Susan received an unexpected call and had to excuse herself due to a work emergency. Before leaving, she asked Doug to serve dessert and ordered them to keep enjoying the evening without her. As she prepared to make her excuses, Noah spoke up.

"Mom made strawberry shortcake."

It was the first time Amanda had heard the boy's voice. She wondered if he appreciated his mother's nonstop talking as much as she and Doug did. Probably not, she figured.

"Strawberry shortcake is my favorite," she said to the boy who smiled with pride. He had his mother's smile. He also had his mother's blond hair, but the blue of his eyes was the same aquamarine as his father's. He'd break hearts for sure.

"Good, I'll go get it, then," Doug announced before he disappeared inside the bungalow. Amanda had seen the house only briefly before being escorted to the back deck with a cold beer, but the little she'd seen had been enough to show her that though modest it was warm and cozy. The kitchen hadn't been updated in at least twenty years. The beige couch dividing the living room from the dining room looked like it was from the same era. So did the huge TV set and the green carpet. Everything seemed clean and in its place, but the couple obviously didn't care about showing off the latest decor and technological advancements.

Doug came back with dessert and three plates and started serving the cake.

"You'll see. My mom's is the best strawberry shortcake ever," Noah said before he attacked his large portion.

"I don't doubt it," Amanda said with a chuckle before she took a smaller bite of her own cake. "Wow. You were not kidding. It's really yummy."

"Told you so," the boy replied with a smile, a dollop of whipped cream on his chin. Amanda glanced at Doug's plate and wasn't surprised to see mostly strawberries covering a thin slice of cake. He ate in silence, letting his son replace his wife as the conversationalist of the house. The situation was somewhat awkward but she enjoyed Noah's enthusiasm. "We're going to the fair this weekend to see the demolition derby. Do you like the demolition derby, Amanda?"

"Ouch, that sounds a little noisy. I think I'll stick to the cows."

"There are plenty of those too, you know. And horses. And tractors! Do you like tractors?"

"Yeah, tractors are awesome," she said to please the boy. His smile made her smile automatically. "There are really big ones, you'll see. I was there last weekend."

"You were? But Dad said you don't have kids."

Doug shifted position in his chair and cleared his throat, obviously uncomfortable with his son's revelation, as if the fact that she didn't have kids was a big secret. "The fair is not only for kids, Noah."

"Did you go alone?" Noah asked, apparently unable to imagine Amanda at the fair for some reason.

"I went with a friend."

"A friend? But Dad said you don't have friends." This time Doug blushed with embarrassment, the red on his face deepening as Amanda burst out in laughter.

"Your dad's right. I don't have many friends because I'm new in Bangor. But I went to the fair with a new friend," she explained to Noah before she turned to Doug. "Joyce Allen. It was her way to thank me for taking care of Dingo. It was a nice gesture."

"Is Dingo a cat?" Noah asked, demanding Amanda's attention back before she could see Doug's reaction. She hadn't thought going out with a client might be an issue until she'd heard herself mention her outing with Joyce to Doug.

"A dog."

"What's wrong with him?"

"He hurt his leg and he needs bandages for a while, but he'll get better."

"Because you fixed him?"

"That's right, in a way," Amanda said with a smile.

"You and my dad are heroes," Noah announced before pushing a large piece of cake into his mouth with his fork. By now whipped cream had made it to his nose.

"If you say so," Amanda said with a giggle as she turned back to Doug, who looked lost in his thoughts. "Is it a problem, Doug?"

He opened his eyes wide and turned to her as if she'd awakened him from a deep sleep. "Huh? What?"

"That I went to the fair with Ms. Allen. Is that a problem?"

"Oh that? No, no, of course not. It's just…"

"What is it, Doug?"

He stared at the strawberries on his plate for what seemed like hours before he finally answered, "I'm surprised you could be friends with a woman like Joyce Allen, that's all." Before Amanda could ask him to explain, he turned to Noah, who'd finished his dessert. "Take your empty plate to the sink and go wash your face, all right? You look like a snowman with whipped cream all over your face like that." Noah laughed at his father's analogy and obeyed, leaving the table with his plate and taking it inside the house. "Sorry, I didn't want him to hear what I'm going to say next. Kids repeat everything, you know."

"I've heard," Amanda agreed, wondering what Doug had to say. She'd never heard him say anything negative about anyone so it had to be important. "So why are you so surprised I could be friends with Joyce Allen?"

"I'm not here to choose your friends, Amanda. Let me be clear on that first and foremost. But I think you should be careful with a woman like Joyce Allen."

"Okay, but why? Not because she's gay, I hope, because…"

"God no," he interrupted. "I hope you know me better than that. I couldn't care less about Joyce Allen's sexuality. Or yours, for that matter," he added before he cleared his throat nervously.

Amanda felt her face heat up, flustered. Doug was apparently a lot more perceptive than she would have guessed. "Good. That's a relief. But what is it then?"

Doug sighed, still hesitant to reveal the information he had, yet evidently wanting to share it with Amanda. He started at last, focused on his plate as he spoke softly to make sure Noah wouldn't hear.

"I sat on a charity committee with Joyce Allen a few years ago. She was there with her wife, Evelyn Graham, and her sister, Barbara Nichols. It was my first charity committee without Susan—she can't say yes to all of them or she'd never be home—and let's say they made my experience hell. I'd never met three women with a snootier or more condescending attitude. They were so judgmental. They judged the families we were there to help as much as they judged the rest of us sitting on the committee. They were there to help their social standing, no one else. That much was clear. We ended up organizing a charity dinner that cost so much money there was almost nothing left for the families that money was meant for. All to put out a show that was up to their standards.

"I was left with a bad taste in my mouth and when Joyce Allen brought her dog to my clinic a year ago I was tempted to tell her to go to hell, but Susan reminded me to be charitable. Apparently she does give a lot of money to organizations Susan volunteers for. But I don't trust her kind, Amanda, and I think you should be careful. She's not the type to be your friend unless she needs something from you. Remember that."

Amanda had never heard Doug talk so much or look so angry. It was a quiet anger, but it was deeply rooted. She couldn't imagine the Joyce Allen he was describing was the same woman who'd taken her to the fair. It didn't add up.

"Thank you for the warning, but I swear the woman you're talking about and the one I know sound like two completely different women. People do change, you know. She lost her wife a few years ago. That's enough to change a person, isn't it?"

Doug looked up from his plate to meet her hopeful gaze. "Maybe. I hope you're right, but be careful anyway. I don't think people that selfish are capable of a complete one-eighty."

"Amanda, do you want to play a video game with me?" Noah had appeared at the patio door with a clean face to make his excited invitation. He seemed eager to play with her and she didn't want to hear more of Doug's stories about Joyce. He'd already succeeded in placing some doubt in her mind and she hated it.

"Yes, of course," she answered as she quickly stood up and left the table. She didn't play video games, but she'd watch Noah for a little while and then she'd leave. She was done talking to Doug for tonight. His intentions were good, but the results of his friendly warning were devastating.

People were so complicated. They had multiple facets, hidden ones even, and one could never know their true motives. If anyone had asked her before tonight if she trusted anyone in this world she would have named Joyce and Doug. Now the two people she thought she could trust exposed two completely opposite versions of Joyce. Who was she supposed to believe? She hated these situations where she had to rely on her intuition. She liked clear instructions, irrefutable facts, everything people would never be with their endless nuances and contradictions.

She'd never truly trusted people before, and as she watched Noah play a video game that didn't make sense to her, she decided she should have stuck to animals. Animals didn't have complicated personalities. They didn't have secrets. They didn't lie. Their needs were clear as water. They ate when they were hungry, slept when they were tired, and when they showed affection you didn't have to wonder if they really loved you or how long it would last. Their love was pure and endless. Of course, the kind of love an animal could provide would never be the kind of love she'd thought she might finally have a chance to find with Joyce. Whether that kind of love was worth risking her peace of mind for remained to be seen.

CHAPTER TWELVE

As Joyce drove in the direction of the Perry Veterinary Clinic on Friday morning, she glanced at the rearview mirror to make sure Dingo was on the backseat. For a second she couldn't remember carrying him to the car and securing his harness. She'd been so happy about seeing Amanda again she'd almost forgotten the true purpose of her visit to the clinic. What would she look like if she showed up for her appointment without Dingo? Fortunately he was there, staring back at her in the mirror with his usual frown. Joyce laughed at her own behavior before she spoke to Dingo. "I'm so sorry, little brat. Your mommy's totally nuts."

Joyce had tried to understand why she was so excited to see Amanda and had attempted to curb her enthusiasm, but even yoga had failed. She was so different from any other friend she'd had in the past thirty years. There was something pure about her, something untainted that made Joyce feel like she could be herself when she was around her. She could dress the way she wanted, speak her mind and laugh as loud as she desired;

Amanda would never judge her. It was refreshing. It was exactly what she needed and wanted in her new life.

When Amanda had confirmed her intuition about her sexuality, Joyce had been both relieved and disappointed. Relieved because Amanda being a lesbian made it that much easier for Joyce to be herself with her, to discuss her past with Evelyn or her dreams for the future. Disappointed because now Barbara would certainly insist that she arrange a meeting between Amanda and Heather.

Joyce wasn't ready to share Amanda. She didn't know her well enough yet, she hadn't had enough of her yet. She wanted to keep her all to herself. So she hadn't called Barbara to share Amanda's coming out with her. She'd decided to wait until she called her or stopped by her house. Every day that went by without having to spill her secret was a day of reprieve.

Joyce arrived at the clinic and carried Dingo inside. She barely had time to sit Dingo on her lap and adjust the pink silk scarf around her neck before Isabelle arrived and asked her to follow her to the exam room. Amanda entered the room shortly afterward and smiled. Joyce saw some restraint in the lovely smile, something she hadn't seen before. "Good morning, Ms. Allen," Amanda said politely. "How is Dingo doing?" Without looking at Joyce, she started scratching Dingo's neck.

Joyce was shocked. She'd expected Amanda to ask how she was doing before she asked about Dingo. They both knew his health was the purpose of this visit, but they were past the client/professional relationship, weren't they? Although that "Ms. Allen" sure sounded businesslike. Maybe Amanda wanted to take a step back. Maybe she wasn't interested in a friendship at all. "He's doing very well. He puts more weight on his leg now. I think he forgets about his splint and bandage," Joyce answered with a nervous chuckle.

"That's very good," Amanda granted. "But don't let him overdo it. He still needs to take it easy for a few weeks, okay?"

"Of course," Joyce agreed as she lowered her eyes to the ground like a young girl who'd been scolded. She was taken aback by Amanda's attitude.

"We'll take Dingo back to remove his bandage now, Ms. Allen, if you don't mind waiting."

"I'd rather watch what you're doing, actually. Like last time. I want to see his leg. Is that possible?"

Amanda finally turned to her and offered her a genuine smile that almost comforted her. The warmer Amanda she knew wasn't far. "Of course, it's possible," she said before she turned to the vet tech. "Isabelle, would you mind going to get scissors and anything else we might need?"

When Isabelle left the room, Joyce didn't waste any time taking advantage of her time alone with Amanda. She had to find out what had caused this change of attitude. "Is something wrong? You seem distant." She placed a hand on Amanda's back and saw the young woman close her eyes and sigh. "I thought we had fun at the fair."

"We did," Amanda admitted as she leaned into Joyce's touch.

"Then what happened? I thought we were becoming friends and this morning you start Ms. Allen'ing me again?"

Amanda turned to Joyce and looked into her eyes. Joyce held her scrutinizing stare even though she felt like she'd been connected to a lie detector. "Why do you really want to be friends with me? Can you answer that question for me? I have nothing to offer you."

"You couldn't be more wrong," Joyce replied. She didn't know what else to say, but Amanda wouldn't let her off the hook so easily.

"Why me?" she asked again.

"I like you. Isn't that enough?"

Isabelle opened the door to the exam room and Joyce dropped her hand to her side. Amanda looked away, freeing her from her intense, interrogating gaze. Joyce didn't know if she'd given the right answer, but it was the truth. She liked Amanda. She really liked her.

"All right, Dingo, let's see what we have here," Amanda said gently as Isabelle helped her lay him on his side on the exam table. Joyce caressed his head and muzzle and whispered calming words to him as she watched Amanda and Isabelle carefully remove the bandage. The smell didn't seem as bad as the first time, but it was definitely still there. So were the sores, although they hadn't worsened. "Shouldn't these be getting better?" she asked anxiously.

"It will be difficult for them to heal properly as long as they're covered with the bandage. We only need to make sure we keep them from getting infected for now. There's no sign of infection so far and I'll give you more antibiotics to keep it that way. Have you noticed if he licks his bandage in those areas? They must be very itchy."

"He tries, but he stops when I ask him."

"That's good, but I think you should use the Elizabethan collar when you're not around and when you go to bed at night. You can't ask him to stop if you don't see him, Joyce," Amanda argued with empathy. Joyce took the use of her first name as a good sign, but she didn't like what Amanda was suggesting.

"Not that plastic cone, please. He's already bandaged and restrained to a stupid crate. I can't put that thing around his neck too. Please, give him a break," she pleaded. She was rewarded with a brief chuckle.

"It's for…"

"For his own good, I know," Joyce grumbled. "I'll try it. I always listen to you, you know."

"Good, keep it that way," Amanda replied with a grin. They finished removing the bandage and Amanda instructed Isabelle to take Dingo back to wash his leg and dry it. "I'll join you in a minute," she added. Isabelle obeyed and as soon as the door closed behind her and Dingo, Amanda turned to Joyce and sighed. "I'm sorry if I seemed cold earlier."

"Does that mean we can be friends?" Joyce asked with a timid, hopeful smile that widened when Amanda nodded.

"We can be friends, but I want to make one thing clear."

"Sure, what is that?"

"I don't play games. If I'm your friend it's because I like you and I enjoy being with you, not because I want to use you in any way for advancement, social standing, or any other crap I couldn't care less about. And I expect the same from you in return. Okay?"

Joyce was confounded by Amanda's warning. She wondered what had happened or what she might have heard about her that made her think this clarification was necessary. She vowed to find out. But for now she only wanted to reassure Amanda.

"That's fair. I don't like games either. I've played them for almost thirty years and I'm done with them. It's obvious you're a straightforward, no-nonsense person and it's one of the reasons why I like you so much."

"That's good."

Amanda's blush and her bashful smile indicated that Joyce had successfully assuaged her worries. Unable to imagine waiting two more weeks to see Amanda again, she took advantage of her win to suggest another outing.

"Now that we're clear on that, what would you think of having breakfast with me tomorrow? At the Bagel Café around ten? My treat." She sensed Amanda's hesitation and quickly added, "We could go for a walk on that trail you like so much afterward. Walk the calories off. What do you say, huh?"

Amanda started laughing quietly at her insistence. "Okay, okay. That does sound like fun. But please tell me you don't really worry about calories." Joyce felt her face heat up as Amanda examined her body from head to toe, a heat that only intensified when she noticed the blush on Amanda's face. Apparently the veterinarian's unexpected appraisal had surprised her as much as it had Joyce.

"Not one bit. I'm too old to worry about my weight," she answered as she waved her hand dismissively in front of her face. She'd felt the need to remind both of them, but especially herself, of their obvious age difference. It was her own way to remember that Amanda couldn't possibly desire her fifty-six-year-old body and she had no right to expect her to.

"Age has nothing to do with it," Amanda replied. "I don't worry about calories either. I eat well and I exercise but I refuse to diet or count calories. It's a waste of time. I'll never be as thin as you are, but that simply means I'm not meant to be. That's how I see it anyway."

"That's very wise," Joyce offered as she intentionally and with difficulty kept herself from looking down at Amanda's hourglass curves, curves she couldn't pretend she hadn't noticed before.

"Well, I better go help Isabelle or you'll never get out of here."

"Yes, of course. So we're on for tomorrow then?"

"Ten o'clock at the Bagel Café. We're on."

"Great. I'll see myself to the waiting room."

"Perfect. We'll come get you when Dingo's ready."

"Thank you."

Amanda nodded and left the exam room. Joyce stayed immobile for a few seconds, wondering if it was the first time she'd had this type of physical reaction to Amanda's appearance. She couldn't deny what she'd felt was attraction, and she was profoundly disturbed by it. Had she been fooling herself in thinking all she wanted from her was friendship? Had she looked at her in a way that made her think she wanted more? Was this morning's warning Amanda's way of asking her to back off?

How humiliating. She wasn't so sure friendship with Amanda was such a good idea anymore, but she couldn't stay away. She would need to be careful around her and make sure the kind of vibes she'd felt this morning didn't flare up again. Ever.

CHAPTER THIRTEEN

Amanda walked on the stone path of Norumbega Parkway, the first of the two beautifully landscaped parks of the Norumbega Mall, an island in the middle of the Kenduskeag Stream. The Mall allowed pedestrians to walk from Franklin Street all the way to Hammond Street. The Norumbega Parkway ended at Central Street, where the Bagel Café was located. It was not even a five-minute walk and Amanda arrived a little before ten. As she waited for Joyce on the sidewalk in front of the popular red brick building, people went inside as others came back out with cups of hot coffee and pastries or bagels. She watched in silence and waited.

It was early August, the morning sun was warm, and she was wearing sandals, shorts, and a T-shirt like most of the people walking by her. Unlike them, however, she had an oversized white sweater on over her T-shirt. She couldn't help it. Ever since she'd started to buy her own clothes as a teenager she'd worn sweaters all year long. Yes, she tended to be cold when most people weren't, but there was more behind her clothing choice.

Her beloved sweaters comforted her. There was something about their heaviness on her body, their long sleeves with which she often covered her hands, the thickness of the knitted fabric she caressed or picked at with her fingers when she was nervous. It was akin to carrying her favorite comfy blanket or a pet with her everywhere.

Amanda glanced at her watch. Joyce was late. Maybe she'd had a chance to reflect about her attitude at the clinic and had decided not to come. She regretted giving Joyce the cold shoulder, but she'd simply been trying to follow Doug's advice. Keeping her distance from her without offering any explanation hadn't been the right way to do it, though.

She knew that, of course, but escaping uncomfortable situations was so much easier than facing them. She'd done it all her life. Joyce could have accepted it, and they would never have seen each other again outside of the clinic. But Joyce had pushed her instead. She'd refused to give up on their friendship so easily, and Amanda was grateful for it now.

She was glad too that she'd expressed her feelings. Joyce had forced her to be honest about her disdain for social games and her absolute refusal to use someone or be used in friendship for any reason. While Doug's warning still bothered her, she wanted to give Joyce the benefit of the doubt. She'd basically admitted being the woman Doug had described. She'd also confirmed that she didn't want to play games anymore. People sometimes claimed they'd changed when it wasn't true, but she was hopeful.

Amanda smiled as the familiar Subaru approached and Joyce waved at her. She'd come. Her heart jumped with joy and relief. She waved back and watched as Joyce stopped her car in a parking spot that had miraculously opened up on the busy street just as Joyce arrived.

She watched admiringly as Joyce walked toward her, her thick, silver hair bouncing and another elegant silk scarf around her neck. This one was royal blue and matched the Capri pants she wore with a white sleeveless blouse. Her appearance was always so impeccable. Amanda felt like a remnant of the grunge era compared to her. Everyone around them seemed to agree, taking in Joyce's natural sophistication while ignoring her. She was virtually invisible. She was okay with that. She wanted to be invisible. That might be difficult, however, once she was seen with Joyce.

"I'm so sorry I'm late. I was fighting with Dingo and that damn Elizabethan collar," Joyce explained as she hugged Amanda.

The sensation of feeling Joyce's body against hers left Amanda paralyzed and unable to return the brief embrace. Her mind was clogged with the mouth-watering smell of her perfume, a delicate combination of flowers and fruit she tried to identify. Rose and apricot, perhaps, but there was more to it. When Joyce's words finally registered, Amanda laughed nervously. "You're late for a good cause then, so you're forgiven."

"I knew you'd understand. Have you been waiting long?"

"About ten minutes, but I was enjoying the morning sun. Don't worry about it, really. It's okay."

"You're kind, thank you. Shall we?" Joyce asked as she extended her arm toward the front door of the restaurant. "I'm starving."

"Of course. Let's go." Amanda hurried to the door and opened it for Joyce, who smiled and gently squeezed her arm to thank her as she walked into the café.

They waited in line for a few minutes and when their turn came Amanda ordered the breakfast sandwich Joyce recommended. Joyce then grabbed the large green tea latte she'd ordered and Amanda followed her with a large black coffee. They sat at one end of a long table sitting eight people. The few times Amanda had visited the café, she'd sat alone with her laptop at the counter lining the front windows. She'd seen other people share the large family-size tables of the café with complete strangers and had thought it would make her uncomfortable. As she sat across from Joyce, however, she found it easy to focus on her and forget that strangers were sitting right next to them.

When their number was called, Joyce asked her to keep an eye on her purse while she went to pick up their food. When Joyce came back she attacked her sandwich with a voracity that clashed with her usual proper manners.

Amanda couldn't help but laugh. "You weren't kidding, were you? You really were starving."

"Oh my god, I'm being a pig, aren't I?" Joyce said as she put the sandwich down and wiped her mouth with a napkin.

"No, please, have at it. It's fun to watch."

They laughed together and Amanda had a bite of her own sandwich. The flavors of the bread, sausage, cheese, and well-seasoned eggs mixed together in ways that exceeded Amanda's expectations. She expressed her pleasure with a moan that surprised her. "Wow, it *is* good."

"Right?"

"Mhm," Amanda offered simply, her mouth already too full to speak again.

They ate in silence for a few more minutes until Joyce put her sandwich down. "I have to slow down," she said before she took a deep breath. Amanda felt her gaze focus on her. "You know what I've realized this morning?"

"No, what is that?" Amanda asked after she swallowed a bite of sandwich nervously.

"I don't even know where you're from. I know you worked in Portland before. Is that where you grew up?"

"No. Boston," Amanda answered. She didn't like talking about her childhood. It wasn't filled with happy memories and she didn't want people to feel bad for her. Of course, Joyce wasn't the type to leave it at that.

"Wow, big city girl, huh? How was it? Tell me about your childhood. Your family."

Amanda sighed, looking for a way to tell Joyce the truth without making it sound as bad as it was. "There isn't much to say. I was raised by a single mother and we didn't have any extended family so I spent a lot of time alone."

"She was working all the time, I imagine. It must have been hard for her to leave you on your own."

Amanda sighed again. She was tempted to simply go with Joyce's hypothesis, but her need to be truthful was stronger. "You could say that. She worked a lot at finding her next drink, high, or boyfriend, that's for sure."

"Oh, Amanda. I'm so sorry," Joyce said as she covered her hand with hers.

Although Amanda enjoyed the touch, Joyce's reaction was exactly what she didn't want. Pity.

"Don't be. I don't feel sorry for myself," she said more defensively than she'd intended. Her tone was abrupt, and she regretted it immediately. Joyce took her hand away, seemingly shocked and hurt by her rude reply. Amanda took a deep breath and spoke with a softer voice. "I'm sorry. I didn't mean to react that way. It's just, you see, I've never wanted people to feel sorry for me. My mother was not a great role model, that's true, but it didn't stop me from achieving my goals. I'm not a sad story."

"Obviously. I mean, you've clearly made quite a success of yourself. But it saddens me to know you had to do it all on your own. I can't help it."

"Thank you, but I'm not the first person to be raised that way and I won't be the last. I don't want anyone's pity, that's all."

"It's not pity, I assure you. It's compassion. And a whole lot of admiration for what you've managed to achieve," Joyce replied with a gentle smile. Her hand was back on Amanda's, warm and comforting.

Amanda closed her eyes, fighting back tears. She cleared her throat before she spoke, but her voice still came out as a rough whisper. "Thank you. I guess I'm not used to compassion."

"Yet you're one of the most compassionate people I've ever met. That in itself is quite an accomplishment, young lady."

She was able to return Joyce's smile this time and felt compelled to tell her more. "I think I owe that to Mrs. Evans. She was in charge of the animal shelter where I started volunteering when I was twelve. I'd heard about it in school and I loved animals. Besides, I needed to get away from home as much as possible. I guess you could say Mrs. Evans took me under her wing. She showed me how to take care of the animals.

She was patient and always found time for me." This time tears escaped and fell to her cheeks and Amanda quickly wiped them away with her napkin.

"Thank god for people like Mrs. Evans," Joyce said softly. "And I bet you owe a lot to those animals too, huh?"

"Oh yes. They were my best friends in the whole wide world. You see, Joyce, I've been blessed in many ways. I don't let my mother define me."

"I do see. And what I see is so very beautiful."

In that moment Amanda melted under the warmth of Joyce's hand and the heat of her eyes. The sensation was as comforting as her thick sweater yet much more gratifying. Her whole being was heated up, but she felt naked, as if she was being seen for the first time. She wanted Joyce to see all of her. So she kept talking, revelling in how easy Joyce made it for her to do so. She lost count of the number of strangers who sat next to them at the large table and left as she talked about her journey to Bangor.

She shared how Mrs. Evans let her watch when the veterinarian came to take care of the shelter's animals and how that experience made her want to go to veterinary school. She talked about how hard she worked in high school to keep her grades up so she could earn the grants she needed for a college education.

"I haven't seen my mom since I left to go to college. To the best of my knowledge she's never made any attempt to contact me. Never responded to my invitation for her to attend my graduation. That's when I gave up."

Joyce listened, mostly. She smiled, nodded, squeezed her hand on a few occasions, but mostly, she listened. And Amanda realized how much she'd needed that.

"I don't know about you, but I'd really like to take that walk now. Maybe not to burn off the calories, but to digest all these emotions," she said with a laugh. She was glad she'd shared so much with Joyce, but she was left feeling bare, stripped of all of her defenses. She needed to move.

"Indeed. Let's go. I've always wanted to try that trail," Joyce agreed without hesitation. They emptied their tray in the trash and recycling bins and left the restaurant. She hadn't been wrong to trust Joyce, Amanda thought. It was so easy to talk to her. So natural. She felt close to her. Too easy? Too natural? Too close?

As they walked through Norumbega Parkway, Joyce stopped in front of the Lady Victory War Memorial. Dedicated to those who died in all wars, it was a beautiful bronze and granite statue of Lady Victory holding two lit torches. She'd stopped to admire the statue many times before, but today she couldn't help but think that a similar memorial could and should be erected for children like Amanda, who succeeded despite the odds, children who hadn't been given the privileges that others like her niece seemed to take for granted.

She glanced at the young woman standing beside her and was filled with pride and affection. The admiration she'd begun to feel for Amanda had multiplied infinitely during their breakfast conversation. Now more than ever she was convinced she was an exceptional woman and she wanted to be in her company as often as she could. She caressed Amanda's shoulder in a caring touch she couldn't keep to herself. They smiled at each other and resumed walking. She fought the urge to hold her hand, to stand even closer to her as they walked side by side. The attraction she felt for her was powerful. But it was not sexual, or so she rationalized. It was the appeal of the hero, like being drawn to an Olympic medalist or a rock star.

"So, what do you think?" Amanda asked, interrupting Joyce's reverie.

Slightly startled, she turned to Amanda, who stood with arms wide open and pivoted slowly, bringing Joyce's attention to their surroundings. "Pretty cool, no?"

"Oh yes, yes, it's beautiful. I almost forgot we were in the city two minutes ago." The sound and feel of the packed dirt and gravel trail under her shoes was so comforting compared to the city sidewalk. The smell of the honey locust and red maple trees that lined up the trail was sweet and invigorating and the melody of the fresh water running down to the Kenduskeag Stream was so relaxing. Joyce enjoyed the walk.

"The trail is about two miles long. I can't wait to see what it looks like in the fall when the leaves change colors. We could come back with Dingo when he's recovered. If you want," Amanda suggested timidly.

"I'd love to. And I'm sure he would too. I do a lot of yoga but I should do this more often. It's an interesting change of scenery."

"There are so many parks around here I want to explore. I usually hike alone but if you and Dingo want to tag along, I'd like that very much."

Amanda's smile was so sweet and inviting. "We will, then. It's actually pretty funny to think I've lived here all my life and you'll be the one introducing me to our hiking trails."

Amanda chuckled and seemed to hesitate before she added, "Maybe we have stuff to teach each other. I would never have gone to the state fair without you. Even sitting at a table with strangers like we did in the café is a challenge for me. You're pushing my boundaries and I think that's good for me."

"Great. I can keep doing that. But tell me if I push too far, okay?"

"Deal."

They exchanged smiles and Joyce wondered if Amanda was as happy as she was at the thought of doing more activities together. They were making indefinite but long-term plans. Joyce's heart beat a little faster as she tried to think of the next adventure she could propose that would take Amanda out of her comfort zone without making her too anxious.

"So," Amanda said, interrupting her thoughts again. "I pretty much bared my soul at the café, but I don't know much about you yet."

"I see where this is going," Joyce said with a laugh. "Ask me anything you want, my dear. I'm an open book." Amanda blushed, obviously embarrassed by the question she wanted to ask. Joyce knew the color on her cheeks wasn't due to the exercise or the heat. She was in great shape—her breathing had barely accelerated despite their rapid pace—and heat didn't affect her if the thick sweater she was still wearing was any indication. She, on the other hand, could feel sweat trickling down her spine and forehead and would have loosened her silk scarf if she wasn't so self conscious about what that might reveal. "Go ahead and ask. Don't be shy," she encouraged Amanda.

"Okay, well, I was hoping you would tell me a little more about Evelyn."

Joyce flinched unexpectedly. For some reason, of all the things she'd imagined Amanda could want to learn more about, Evelyn had never been an option. She felt awkward bringing her wife into a conversation with Amanda, although she couldn't explain why. "Evelyn. Okay. What about her would you like to know?"

"Anything you want to share. What kind of woman was she? How did you meet?"

Joyce laughed, going back to the holiday office party where Evelyn had first spoken to her. "She saved me from Dan Murdoch." Joyce turned to Amanda, who squinted at her, confused. "I'd been hired at the bank in November so when I went to the holiday party I didn't know anyone besides the people I worked with every day. This guy, Dan Murdoch, kept asking me to dance with him. The drunker he got the more insistent he became. He was such a sleaze."

"So Evelyn came to the rescue and asked you to dance?" Amanda offered.

"Oh god no. We were together for over twenty years before we finally came out at the office. Things were different back then, you know." Amanda nodded. "So no, Evelyn didn't ask me to dance. But she and Dan's wife were old high school friends, so Evelyn called her and said Dan had too much to drink and was making an ass of himself. Mrs. Murdoch came and dragged Dan out of the party in no time. I was so relieved."

"But how did you find out Evelyn was behind it?"

"Oh, she made sure to tell me. A few minutes after Dan left with his wife Evelyn walked up to me and announced that he wouldn't be bothering me anymore. She winked at me to make sure I understood. She was tall and handsome and so charming. After that she invited me to a few parties at her house. There were only women at her parties, of course, and I quickly understood what it was all about. Evelyn only had eyes for me though, and it didn't take long before I moved in with her. We were together for twenty-eight years until…"

"She passed away," Amanda said softly.

"Yes."

"That's so sad."

"It was. But we had so many wonderful years. We built a comfortable life together. And death is how lasting love ends in real life, unfortunately. Nothing like books or movies." Joyce looked to the sky to battle threatening tears and took a deep breath. When she looked at Amanda again, she hoped her smile was convincing. Talking about Evelyn still hurt.

"You loved her very much. It shows," Amanda whispered as she briefly placed her hand on Joyce's lower back. The touch was hesitant but comforting.

"Very much indeed. She was my first love. My only love." Joyce took another breath before she added, "But toward the end I didn't love myself that much." Her revelation shocked her as much as it did Amanda. She never shared that part of her story with anyone before, not even Barbara.

"What do you mean?"

"I let Evelyn make all the decisions in our life. I became a proper woman with proper social standing, living in the proper neighborhood and doing all the proper activities, but I knew that wasn't really me. Even though I didn't know who the real me was, I knew *that* wasn't it. Since Evelyn's death I've been trying to connect with the person I really want to be. It's a long process," she explained. She turned to Amanda and smiled timidly. "You know I've never admitted that to anyone before now? They wouldn't understand. Especially my sister. She and Evelyn had a lot in common."

Amanda smiled in return and placed her hand on Joyce's back again. This time her touch was firmer and lasted longer. "Well, I'm glad you trust me enough to share this with me. I think it's important to find out who you really are and want to be, even if it's a long process. I know who I am and I've known for a long time, but I've always stayed away from social expectations and obligations. I think they tend to complicate things."

Joyce laughed out loud. "You're so right. And so wise. It seems like you've understood at a very young age things I'm barely beginning to understand now. It's amazing." Amanda blushed and smiled with pride at the compliment. Joyce gently took hold of her arm, forcing them to walk closer together. She couldn't resist the pull any longer. They'd shared too much. "I think that's why I'm telling you all of this. Somehow I have a feeling you have an important role to play in my process."

"Oh? And what role would that be?"

"I'm not sure yet. It's just a feeling I have."

"I see."

They walked all the way to the end of the trail and turned around. As they approached Franklin Street and the inevitable end of their time together, Joyce felt the urge to make plans for their next outing. Something fun and exciting. Something Amanda wouldn't think of doing on her own. And idea flashed through her mind. "What are you doing next Saturday?"

"I had nothing planned, but I'm guessing you have something in mind," Amanda said with an enthusiastic smile.

"I do. Something I bet you've never done."

"I don't doubt it. What is it?"

"Did you know there's a casino in Bangor?"

"A casino?" Amanda's expression became of mix of fear and excitement.

"Yes. A casino. We'll have so much fun. Say yes." Amanda laughed louder than she usually did, which she took as encouragement. She stopped walking and took a hold of Amanda's shoulders, forcing her to look into her eyes. "Come on. Say yes."

"Yes. As if I could say anything else."

"Good girl. You won't regret it." Joyce threw her arms around Amanda's shoulders and hugged her.

She was stunned when Amanda hugged her back, her strong arms closing around her waist and pulling her tight against her body. The long embrace marked a new level of intimacy in their friendship, and Joyce allowed herself to get lost in the younger woman's arms until Amanda pulled away. As they walked the rest of the way to Amanda's building, she caught herself hoping she would invite her upstairs. She couldn't bring herself to say goodbye.

That's exactly what she did though. She told Amanda she'd call her to make definite plans for their adventure at the casino and Amanda disappeared into the condominium complex, leaving her alone on the sidewalk with a heart that felt both light and heavy all at once.

CHAPTER FOURTEEN

Holding the Upward-Facing Dog Pose—her favorite—Joyce tried to focus on her breathing. Every summer morning, unless it rained, she took her yoga mat outside to the backyard. The view there of the Penobscot River was as serene as it was breathtaking and she was convinced the fresh air made her breathing exercises even more beneficial. Today, however, the view and fresh air didn't seem to be helping her control her own thoughts. She switched positions and sat in the Perfect Pose, legs crossed, hands open and wrists resting on her knees. She closed her eyes and tried to center her energy, but she was distracted when she heard Dingo sigh loudly. Looking to her left, she saw that he was on his side in the middle of his dog pen, sunbathing.

Dingo also enjoyed their time outside. She'd purchased the dog pen so she could bring him out to the backyard with her without having to hold his leash. Even with his injured leg, she didn't trust him not to run away. The pen measured eight feet by six feet, large enough for him to explore without overdoing it and sniff all the grass he wanted before he lay back down. She regretted the fact that she would no longer be able to use it once he recovered. As soon as his leg was back to normal, he would easily jump over its four-foot-high walls. They would need to resume their daily trips to the park then or go explore hiking trails with Amanda. She smiled at the thought. "You will love that, little brat. You'll see." She sighed with frustration.

No matter what she tried, her thoughts always went back to Amanda. Her eyes or her smile would flash through her mind or she'd remember something she'd said. The trees reminded her of the walk they'd shared. And Dingo, well, of course she thought of Amanda every time she looked at his leg.

"There you are! I've been knocking at the front door for ten minutes," Barbara yelled from the back porch. "I decided to let myself in. You should really lock your door, you know," she continued without any regard for Joyce's obvious meditation pose.

Joyce sighed again. Oh well, it wasn't like she was going to reach inner peace this morning anyway. "Hi Barb, how are you doing on this beautiful Wednesday morning?" she asked as she rolled up her yoga mat.

"Terrible. I've been crazy busy organizing this gala for the chamber of commerce. I could use your help, you know."

"Not interested. I've told you already." Joyce left the yoga mat on the porch and grabbed the silk scarf she'd left there, quickly rolling it around her neck, sensing that Barbara was staring at her neck the entire time. She knew Joyce wore them to hide her neck and had supported her decision to do so. While Joyce would never mention her sister's wrinkles to spare her feelings, Barbara never missed a chance to remind her of her flaws. She was judgmental to the bone. Joyce hated herself for being so self-conscious around her sister, whose designer skirt and blazer contrasted with her own yoga pants and tank top. How she longed for the day she wouldn't care what Barbara thought of her attire. Would that day ever come?

She went to carry Dingo out of the pen and came back to the porch to face Barbara, arms crossed on her chest. "You really won't help me?" she asked, a look of disapproval on her face.

"My days organizing any kind of fancy event are over, sis. I won't change my mind. I'm not even attending them anymore," she explained for the thousandth time as she walked past Barbara through the patio door her sister had left open. She put Dingo down on his dog bed and handed him his favorite toy before she turned back to Barbara, who'd followed her inside.

"That's very selfish of you," Barbara spat out.

"Perhaps, but that's the way it is."

"God, Joy, have you listened to yourself lately? You sound like Heather when she was a teenager. Are you going through some kind of midlife crisis?"

"I'm pretty sure I'm past midlife, but call it what you want. I won't let you or anyone else dictate my schedule anymore. Would you like a mimosa?"

"All right, all right, I'll stop trying to convince you. And yes, please. But go easy on the orange juice."

Joyce didn't feel guilty for using alcohol to divert Barbara's mind. She'd helped her organize so many events in the past that she'd lost count. It was a boring and time-consuming task that required her to spend time with people from her former life. She wasn't going back, not even to help her sister.

They went to the kitchen where Joyce grabbed two champagne flutes out of the cupboards, orange juice from the fridge, and a bottle of sparkling wine from the wine cooler. She made a mental note to stock up on wine the next time she went to the store. Barbara took her usual spot at the breakfast bar and whined about the list of errands she had to run today. She didn't stop until Joyce handed her a mimosa. "But I couldn't get anything started before I stopped by to see you. It's been a while. I haven't seen you since your outing with Dingo's vet."

"I know. I figured you were busy," Joyce stopped short of adding that she had no complaints. She knew all too well what Barbara had finally showed up to find out.

"So?"

"So what?" she asked, pretending she didn't know what her sister was asking.

"Joyce Allen, you'll be the death of me. Quit acting stupid, it doesn't suit you. Is our young veterinarian a lesbian, yes or no?"

Never had Joyce been so tempted to lie. She desperately wanted to keep Amanda's sexuality a secret so she could keep her all to herself. Just a little longer. If she introduced Amanda to Heather and a flame sparked between them, Amanda wouldn't have time for Joyce anymore. And if things didn't go well and Amanda ended up getting hurt, she might blame Joyce for her broken heart. Either way she lost. How much she'd lose was all that remained to be seen. She didn't want to get involved in this mess, yet she couldn't lie to her sister. "She's gay, but I don't think she's Heather's type."

"Duh. Of course she's not Heather's type. She has a brain. Our goal here is precisely to make Heather fall for someone who's *not* her type. Have you forgotten?"

"That's *your* goal, Barb, not mine. I don't see why Heather would suddenly fall for someone like Amanda if she's never fallen for intelligent and independent women before. Do you think her aunt setting up this blind date will be that much of a turn-on for Heather? Because I, for one, really don't think so."

"Oh Joy, my dear sister, how you underestimate me. You're right. If Heather smells so much as a hint of a setup, she'll never go for it. But she'll never know we're trying to set her up." She tapped the side of her head with her index finger. She had a plan. "I have it all figured out, trust me. But for this to work, I have to make sure of one thing first. Is your vet at least moderately good-looking?"

Joyce couldn't help but smile and she hoped she wasn't blushing. "She's gorgeous. She's definitely not a bimbo like most of Heather's girlfriends, but she's undeniably beautiful."

"Good. As long as she's somewhat attractive, that's all we need for Heather to like her. God, that's sad. So here's what we're going to do. You'll have me, Heather, and Amanda for dinner here Saturday night."

"Don't you think Heather will suspect something if Amanda's here for dinner? Why would I invite my new friend to have dinner with my sister and my niece? It doesn't make sense."

"Hear me out. Heather won't suspect a thing. Because your invitation was officially for Sunday night." She made air quotation marks with her fingers. "But you know me and my forgetful mind, right? Especially with that gala to organize, I can't keep track of things. I'll tell Heather the invitation was for Saturday and we'll show up a day early." Barbara winked and grinned mischievously.

"That's a big mix-up, Barb, even for you. I don't think she'll fall for it."

"Don't forget you're talking about me, here. The same woman who showed up a week early for her last doctor's appointment. The same woman who called her daughter in a panic over having her car stolen at the mall until said daughter reminded me she'd dropped me off at the mall and kept the car. The same…"

"Okay, okay, I get it. You've completely lost your mind. I remember now."

"Hey now, watch it."

Joyce laughed until she realized what Barbara was asking her to do. She was expected to invite Amanda to her house without telling her Barbara and Heather would join them. "So wait, you want me to trick Heather *and* Amanda? I can't do that. Amanda is very anxious around new people. I can't trap her like that."

"Oh yes, you can, and you will if you love me, dear sister. Amanda will get over it when she's in Heather's arms. They all fall for her. You know it's true. She'll thank you, trust me."

Yes, all women seemed to find Heather irresistible, but somehow Joyce didn't think Amanda would ever be grateful for being tricked into a blind date. It didn't seem possible. Even if she did fall in love with Heather, which she couldn't imagine without getting knots in her stomach. "I'm not convinced. Besides, I can't this Saturday anyway. I have plans."

"Next Saturday then? I beg you, help me find a good prospect for my daughter, for your goddaughter. Please."

"I'll think about it," Joyce answered. She figured it was easier to postpone the discussion than to argue about Barbara's ploy for the next twenty minutes.

"I knew you'd do it," Barbara said before she emptied her glass, grabbed her purse, and walked around the breakfast bar to lay a loud smack on Joyce's cheek.

"I didn't say I'd do it. I said I'd think about it."

"Whatever you say. I've got to run now, but I'll call you."

Joyce followed Barbara to the front door and closed it behind her. She leaned against the closed door and sighed heavily. She then went to the living room and picked up Dingo from his dog bed. She needed some kind of comfort. "How am I going to get out of this, Dingo? There's no way I can do this to Amanda." Dingo licked her cheek before he laid his muzzle on her shoulder. "What have I done to the universe to get stuck with such a manipulative sister?"

CHAPTER FIFTEEN

Joyce picked up Amanda at her apartment at four p.m., and they drove to the casino. Amanda was more excited about seeing her than she was nervous about the casino crowd until Joyce stopped the engine of her Subaru in the parking garage. Her breathing became shallow, her hands cold and damp. She closed her eyes to focus on taking deep breaths, and she felt Joyce's hand on hers. "Are you okay?"

"No, but I'll get there. Just give me a minute," she said through heavy breaths as she turned toward Joyce and smiled weakly. She hated that she was putting her through this again, which made her even more anxious. She didn't want her to regret taking her to the casino. She really wanted to go, but she needed a moment to calm down. Staring into her peaceful, carbon eyes, was helpful. Joyce looked at her in the eye, as if she knew she had a calming effect on her.

Joyce was dressed even more elegantly than usual. She wore a light blue sleeveless dress that ended above the knees with a long, darker blue vest, also sleeveless, over it. Her silk scarf was the same dark blue as the vest. Impeccable makeup and a beautiful yet simple silver bracelet completed the look.

Amanda felt underdressed with her own black Capri pants, black tank top, and dark gray sweater. She also felt self-conscious about her same old ponytail. She started to lose control of her nerves again and had to remind herself that fashion was merely another social game she refused to play. She hoped Joyce didn't mind.

Joyce held her gaze and gently rubbed her hand to comfort her. "I have an idea," she said. "Why don't we go pay our respects to Paul Bunyan before we go in? The fresh air will do us good."

"Paul Bunyan?" Amanda asked, puzzled. She didn't know who Paul Bunyan was, but she doubted being introduced to a stranger now would help calm her in any way.

"Yes, Paul Bunyan. The legendary lumberjack. We have a giant statue of him on Main Street. It's not even a five-minute walk. Don't tell me you haven't paid a visit to Paul yet."

Amanda sighed with relief and even chuckled. *A giant statue*, she repeated to herself. Joyce had a way to lighten up the most anxiety-provoking of situations. "I haven't."

"Oh my god, Amanda. That's a sacrilege. Let's go right now. You have to meet the man." Amanda laughed more freely and felt herself relax as she watched Joyce walk around the car to open her door. "What are you waiting for? Let's go."

"Right now? You're serious?"

"Of course I'm serious. You can't live in Bangor without knowing about the giant lumberjack and being properly introduced to him, young lady. Besides, he'll bring us luck." She winked and Amanda accepted the hand she offered to help her out of the car.

The fresh air outside of the parking garage soothed her almost immediately. The walk that took them to the giant statue of Paul Bunyan might indeed be very short, yet Amanda wondered how Joyce managed to walk in heels that appeared to be at least four inches high. She moved along as fast and easily as Amanda did with her Keen slip-ons. Of course, the length of her legs probably helped her keep up the pace.

It didn't take long before they saw the statue. Amanda didn't dare laugh but the statue did seem funny from a distance. The bright green of the lumberjack's pants, the red and black of the plaid shirt, and the smiling bearded face all seemed too cheerful and colorful at first glance, as if the statue belonged in Disney World rather than in downtown Bangor.

"You'll learn to love it," Joyce said next to her, as if she'd read her expression. "Might as well," she added with a wink. "It's not going anywhere."

"It's huge. Pretty impressive," Amanda admitted as they got closer.

"It's thirty-one feet tall. And it's made of metal and fiberglass. It was given to Bangor by a group of New York builders in 1959, two years before I was born. I grew up with it. I loved it when I was a little girl. I found it so imposing. And I was fascinated when my dad told me there's a time capsule in the base."

"Really?"

"Yes. But I doubt we'll be around when they open it."

"When will that be?"

"2084," Joyce answered as she examined Amanda. "Come to think of it, you might still be around," she added with a smile.

Amanda didn't want to think of a time when she might have to live without Joyce in her life. The realization scared her. She'd never feared anyone's death before, not even her mother's. How did people live with the threat of losing the ones they loved? She assumed it was the price to pay for letting herself get close to anyone. She didn't like how vulnerable it made her feel, but she couldn't go back now. The time she spent with Joyce was too precious. "If I'm around I'll find a way to tell you what was in the capsule, don't worry."

Joyce smiled and leaned against the base of the statue. "Is that a promise?"

"It is," Amanda said as she leaned next to her, close enough for their arms to touch.

"The funny thing is I don't doubt you'll find a way to keep that promise. You're a special kind of woman," Joyce said softly before she bumped Amanda's hip with her own and straightened up to face her. "Are you feeling better now?"

"I am, thank you. The fresh air worked."

"It's the lumberjack, dear."

"Oh yeah, of course. It's all thanks to Paul."

They laughed and Joyce offered her hand again, this time to pull Amanda from the statue and start walking toward the casino. "Okay then, now that we've touched him, Lady Luck will be with us."

As they walked side by side Amanda couldn't stop thinking about death and how it could so cruelly separate people from their loved ones.

"How did you do it, Joyce? After Evelyn passed away. How did you find a way to go on?" She covered her mouth with her hand as soon as she realized what she'd said. "Oh god, I'm so sorry. You don't have to answer that. It's a very personal question, I know."

Joyce frowned briefly, clearly taken by surprise, but then she turned to Amanda and smiled. "No, it's okay. It's personal, yes, but I don't expect superficial from you." After a few more steps, she continued, "It wasn't easy. I was deeply depressed for several months. I even thought I wanted to die. And then I started to learn how to be alone."

"How did you do that?"

"I made conscious efforts to reconnect with myself. I told you last time I didn't like the person I'd become toward the end of my relationship with Evelyn. Well, finding myself alone forced me to face that fact and to take steps toward discovering who I truly am and want to be."

"But how?" Amanda felt compelled to ask.

Joyce laughed. "You remind me of my niece when she was a little girl. One answer inevitably brought up another question."

"I'm sorry. I don't mean to pry," Amanda said as she lowered her gaze to the ground. She wanted to find out so much more, but she had to give Joyce some space.

"You're not prying. It's okay. You're genuinely interested, and that's a nice change. Don't be afraid to ask. If you go too far I'll tell you."

"Okay, good." She took a deep breath. "So tell me, how did you get started on that process?"

"First I retired. Evelyn and I worked at the bank together—we met there as you know—and I couldn't move forward while I kept working there. Everything in that place was her, not me." She paused to look at Amanda, who nodded her understanding. Then she smiled tenderly. "Once I retired, I adopted Dingo. I've always wanted a dog and Evelyn didn't, so that was the first logical step. I needed a dog in my life. And I needed the company."

"They do make great companions."

"Oh yes. I never regretted adopting him. In fact, every time I look at him I'm grateful he's in my life. Even if that injured leg of his is costing me a fortune." She laughed and turned to Amanda again. "Besides, without him I wouldn't have met you."

Amanda looked to the ground again as she felt her cheeks heat up. She wanted to tell Joyce how happy she was that they'd met too, but she couldn't find the right words, so she kept her line of questioning instead.

"And then? After you adopted Dingo, what else did you do to find your true self?"

"Well, then I took classes."

"What kind of classes?"

Joyce laughed and shook her head, almost embarrassed. "Everything. Painting, yoga, numerology, pottery, piano…I tried so many things that I lost count. I also read a lot of self-help books, but I found they all sounded the same in the end. Classes were more fun, more interactive, and they allowed me to experience new things and discover different facets of myself."

"Did you like any of them more than others? Did anything stick?"

"I still do yoga every day, and I paint every chance I get. Painting was an old love of mine. One I'd forgotten and was glad to rediscover."

"The Creative Child," Amanda said, remembering the first day they'd met. Joyce turned to her with a puzzled expression until she finally remembered talking with her about numerology and smiled.

"That's right. Born on March third. Double three. We make quite a pair, you know, you and me. The Seeker and The Creative Child. With curiosity and creativity we could get through just about anything, don't you think?"

"I do," Amanda confirmed with a smile. The more she learned about Joyce's journey the more she admired her. She'd managed to mourn her wife and come out of it stronger, with a newfound will to learn and to better herself.

"I hope I get to see your paintings some day," she said. She wondered what Joyce's favorite subjects were, what her style was, what medium she used, which colors were her favorites.

"I'm sure you will eventually," Joyce assured as they came to the casino entrance. "But for now, are you ready to win big bucks?"

Amanda nodded and took a deep breath. She was calm and ready to face the crowd. With Joyce.

"Win or lose, I'm ready. Let's go in." Joyce opened the door for her and let her walk into the building first, placing hand on her lower back to encourage her forward.

Joyce remained close to Amanda as they moved into the casino crowd. She seemed nervous, but there was no sign of panic yet. She was taking in the scene, studying the numerous slot machines and game tables. As she watched, she saw her briefly cup her hand over one ear, adjusting to the sounds that were bombarding them. It was obvious she'd never been to a casino before. Joyce personally enjoyed the sound the slot machines made and how it mixed with the music coming at them from everywhere. It didn't harmonize, but the cacophony gave Joyce a unique kind of rush. She wasn't a compulsive gambler, but she had fun visiting the place once in a while. She hoped Amanda would have fun too.

Joyce couldn't believe how much she'd opened up to Amanda. She'd never before told anyone that healing from the loss of her wife had involved evolving as a person who was markedly different from the one Evelyn had been married to. How could she? She still had a hard time admitting it to herself. Finding anything positive in her wife's death was a form of betrayal, wasn't it? Maybe she'd be able to move beyond that guilt as she continued to confide in Amanda. She didn't know if she found it easier to talk to her because she hadn't known Evelyn or simply because of the way she was, but she knew she could count on her to help her work through her feelings of culpability.

"So, what do you think of the place?" she asked Amanda, who was still carefully studying her surroundings.

"It's noisy, and it's crowded, but it's completely new and kind of exciting," Amanda explained with a hesitant smile. "Don't leave me alone though. It looks like a labyrinth in here."

Joyce laughed. She'd gotten lost in the maze of slot machines in the past so she knew Amanda wasn't wrong to be worried. "I'm sticking to you like glue, don't worry. Where would you like to start?"

Amanda shrugged. "I don't know. I have no idea how any of these machines work. I'll observe you for a little while if that's okay."

"Excellent. Let's start at the blackjack table, shall we?"

Amanda followed her to a table covered in green velvet where one seat was available. She sat on the stool and bought some chips from the dealer. Blackjack was her favorite game although she always seemed to ask the dealer to hit her with one card too many, going bust every time. Or almost every time. The rare occasion she hit the perfect twenty-one kept her coming back.

Amanda stood behind her, looking over her shoulder. She was so close she could feel her breath on her neck. Warm breath that penetrated the silk of her scarf to her skin. The sensation gave Joyce chills. It was distracting, but sensual. Much too sensual.

To make things worse, people were continually walking by, forcing Amanda to press her body into Joyce's back. She felt guilty about the pleasure she took from that. It made her so uncomfortable, in fact, that after just a few losing hands she grabbed her remaining chips and stood up from her stool. "This is boring for you," she said. "You don't get to play at all. Let's try some slots instead, okay?"

"It wasn't boring, I assure you," Amanda replied, her face flushed. "But it is a little tight here."

"Right. Let's go somewhere we can breathe better." Joyce took her hand and guided her through the crowd gathered around the game tables. She dropped her hand once they had more room to maneuver, but Amanda remained close, following her through the alleys of slot machines. She finally spotted two machines side-by-side that appeared interesting. She sat in front of the first machine and patted the seat next to her so Amanda would sit.

Amanda looked up at the tall illuminated display screen, obviously intimidated. "How does this work?"

Amused, Joyce explained where to insert money and how to choose the amount of each bet. "That's about it. There's no science here. It's purely random."

"Okay. If you say so." Amanda played reluctantly at first, but then her machine started paying small amounts here and there and she laughed gleefully every time the music announcing a gain started playing.

Joyce's own machine didn't pay out a dime so she waited a few minutes between each bet so she could make her money last longer and not lose her seat next to Amanda. Watching her enjoy herself this much was too much fun. Joyce laughed. She'd hoped Amanda would enjoy going to the casino, but she'd never imagined she could play with such abandon, even grabbing Joyce by the neck and hugging her when she accessed a bonus round. She was beginning to fear she might have created a monster when Amanda declared that she was hungry.

"All right. There's a pub right here in the casino. We can have a bite before we leave. They have excellent beer."

"Sounds good. One last bet and we're going, okay?"

Joyce nodded and watched as Amanda shockingly selected the maximum bet of four dollars. "Let's make it count."

"You're crazy," Joyce said before she laughed. The animated wheels started spinning and Amanda grabbed her hand and squeezed it tight. Dragon figures lined up on the screen and the winning music started playing as the words "big win" flashed on the screen. "Oh my god, Amanda, you've won five hundred dollars!"

"What? Holy shit!"

Joyce laughed out loud. She'd never before heard Amanda cuss. She was so excited she hugged Joyce again.

"All right, let's go now. I'm buying dinner," Amanda announced.

"You better," Joyce said with a wink before she hit a button on Amanda's machine and a ticket printed out.

"Thank you, Joyce. For bringing me here. It was such a blast. I have so much fun with you," Amanda said as a blush covered her face.

There was no doubt in Joyce's mind the young woman was genuinely grateful and she found that making her this happy for a couple of hours was unexpectedly gratifying to her as well. "You're welcome. Now let's go cash in your money and get something to eat."

Minutes later they were sitting at a small table sharing onion rings and chicken wings and drinking craft beer. Amanda was only halfway through hers when her eyes became glassy. "You're not a big drinker, are you?" Joyce asked teasingly.

"It's obvious isn't it? I never drink. But today is a special day."

"I'll drink to that." They clanked their glasses together and took another sip of beer.

Joyce enjoyed watching Amanda loosen up and enjoy herself, but she had to admit she wasn't the only one having a good time. She hadn't felt this relaxed and comfortable in anyone's company in a very long time. She hoped the feeling was mutual. The thought made her realize that although she'd divulged a lot about Evelyn already, Amanda had never talked about her love life. Perhaps thanks to the beer, she dared to bring it up. "You know, I was wondering about something." She paused to see if Amanda would encourage her to continue.

"About what?" Amanda prompted innocently, opening the door for her.

"Well, you've asked a lot of questions about my relationship with Evelyn, but what about you? Have you ever been in love?"

Amanda didn't stiffen up as Joyce had feared, but she lowered her gaze to her drink and focused on wiping droplets of condensation on her glass for several seconds before she finally shook her head. "No, never. I had a crush on a professor once, but nothing serious."

"That's such a shame," Joyce said before she could stop herself. "You're such a bright, beautiful, and kind young woman. You have so much to offer."

"I've always been scared to let anyone in. Scared of being hurt. But lately..." She didn't finish her thought.

"Lately?" Joyce asked, urging her to continue.

Amanda leaned over the table and met her gaze. She was clearly getting tipsy, but there was a new, self-assured expression in her eyes that was almost seductive. "But lately I've been thinking I might be ready, you know, for that kind of love in my life. I mean, to share my life with a woman I love and who loves me for who I am. I'd never thought it could happen for me before..." Her voice trailed off again and she dropped her eyes to the glass of beer she was holding.

"Before what?" Joyce insisted.

"Before I met you," Amanda declared without looking at her.

Joyce's heart started racing uncontrollably, even as she told herself that it was hearing about her relationship with Evelyn that had most likely taught Amanda that love could last. She was glad she was able to convince the young woman that even when it hurt, love was still worth it. If their friendship had allowed Amanda to open up to love, that was something to be proud of.

"Well, I hope you do find love, my dear. Any young woman would be lucky to be loved by you."

Amanda looked up and Joyce thought she saw a flash of sadness pass through her eyes before she looked down again and sighed. They changed the subject to lighter topics, but as they chatted Joyce wondered what she could do to help Amanda find love.

She gave some more thought to the scheme Barbara had proposed on Wednesday. She'd had no intention of helping her with it. Until now, that is. Maybe—if she put her own feelings aside, her own fear of losing Amanda's attention—it might not be such a bad idea to introduce her to Heather. Perhaps Heather could be the woman she deserved. And if she couldn't, Heather knew other women their age that Amanda might be interested in.

Perhaps the right, unselfish thing to do was to go along with Barbara after all. She vowed to consider the option again. Later. Now, however, she was going to focus on enjoying her time with Amanda—while she still had her full attention.

CHAPTER SIXTEEN

"All right. Let's take a look at that leg," Amanda said with a grin before she forced her attention away from Joyce and onto Dingo. She put him in a standing position on the exam table to observe how much weight he put on his bandaged leg. He stood proudly, as if he didn't have a bandage at all. Satisfied with what she saw, she scratched the dog's neck and smiled at Joyce.

She hadn't seen her or spoken to her all week and she'd missed her terribly. And she'd worried. She'd relived their time at the casino and their conversations over and over again since then and although most of her memories made her smile, the part about her own love life left her embarrassed.

She regretted telling Joyce that she felt ready to find love since she'd met her. The beer had made it easy to offer what she'd thought could only be interpreted as a proclamation of her romantic interest in Joyce. But she hadn't responded the way she'd hoped. She'd obviously misunderstood her confession or, worse, had acted like she didn't understand because she wasn't interested. Either way Amanda had feared that she'd scared her away and lost her friendship. She was relieved to see her appear to be as comfortable in her presence this morning as she'd been last Saturday.

"Well, that looks really good. If all is going as planned today should be the last time we use a splint. The next bandage will be a soft one. Do you have any concerns?"

"No. He's doing very well. It's getting harder to limit exercise though. He wants to run so badly. I don't think he realizes he still has a while to go before he fully recovers from his injury," Joyce said with a chuckle Amanda found so sweet she couldn't help but join in her laughter.

"That's a good sign." Her gaze lingered on Joyce's dark eyes.

"Should I go get the scissors?" Isabelle asked, reminding Amanda of her presence in the exam room.

"Yes," Amanda said before she cleared her throat and turned to the vet tech. "Yes, that would be great. Thank you." Isabelle left the room and Amanda brought her attention back to Joyce. "Did you have a good week?"

"Yes, I did, thank you. Did you?"

"Yes. Thank you again for last Saturday. It was really nice." She wanted to say so much more, but didn't know where to start. She petted Dingo vigorously, grateful to be able to plunge her fingers into his fur so she could work out some of her nerves. Dingo had no complaint, enjoying the massage.

"No need to thank me. I enjoyed it too. I almost called you this week to go for coffee but I didn't dare," Joyce said, uncharacteristically hesitant.

"You should have," Amanda replied a little too enthusiastically before Isabelle came back with the scissors.

Amanda focused on her work, not looking at Joyce again before Dingo's leg was exposed. "The sores aren't infected and there aren't any new ones, so we're on the right track," she explained with a quick reassuring smile to Joyce, who was studying his leg with an endearing, concerned expression on her face. "We're still going to clean his leg and dry it well before we replace the bandage."

"Yes, I know the drill," Joyce replied with a laugh. "I'll sit in the waiting room."

"Great, we'll be with you as soon as he's ready." Amanda's heart ached when she watched her leave the exam room. She'd been waiting six days to see Joyce again and they hadn't been able to share anything meaningful. This kind of polite and superficial chitchat was so unsatisfying after the much deeper conversations they'd shared recently. Amanda followed Isabelle to the back room with Dingo in her arms, wondering why Joyce hadn't called. She was usually more talkative and didn't shy away from proposing outings. What had stopped her this time? She needed to talk to her again. This meeting had been a lot more frustrating than satisfying.

As Joyce sat patiently in the waiting room, she pondered her decision to invite Amanda to her house for dinner the following day. After their evening at the casino, she'd concluded that she'd been selfish in her decision to keep her to herself. Amanda had confided that she wanted to find love and Joyce had the power to help her meet women her own age with whom she might develop a romantic relationship. All she had to do was introduce Amanda to Heather. If there were no fireworks between them, Amanda would more than likely find someone else within Heather's wide circle of friends.

Joyce had convinced herself it was the right thing to do, yet she'd postponed making the invitation. She didn't like the idea of tricking Amanda into meeting her niece, and she hated the idea of sharing her with Heather even more.

Feeling someone approach, she looked up. She was surprised to see Amanda instead of Isabelle, holding Dingo in her arms. "I'll walk you to your car," she announced with a smile.

"Wow, that's going above and beyond your call of duty, isn't it, Doctor Carter?"

"Perhaps, but I do it for all my favorite clients," Amanda whispered.

Joyce laughed as quietly as she could. She'd already paid for the visit and the antibiotics she carried in her purse so she proceeded to the front door of the clinic and held it open for Amanda, who was still carrying Dingo. They walked toward her Subaru in silence and installed him in the backseat.

"Thank you," Joyce said before she started to open the driver's door of her car. Somehow her invitation to dinner was still stuck in the back of her throat. Before she could open the door wide enough to get in, however, Amanda stopped her.

"Wait."

Joyce turned to Amanda and saw that a dark, uneven blush had covered her face. She was obviously nervous about something. She closed the car door and gave Amanda her full attention, stopping short of taking her hands because they were standing in front of the clinic. "What is it?"

"Actually, I walked out here with you because I wanted a little bit more time to…" Her voice trailed off. Joyce offered an encouraging smile as she waited, finding it more and more difficult not to give Amanda any kind of physical comfort as she struggled to express her thoughts. At last, the beautiful redhead took a deep breath and went on, "Well, I was hoping we could do something this weekend, if you're available. I'd hate to wait until Dingo's next appointment to see you again."

Joyce stared into Amanda's soft brandy-brown eyes and sighed, resigned. It was time to take Amanda and herself out of their misery. "I'd hate that too. Very much so. In fact, I was hoping you might join me and Dingo for dinner at our house tomorrow. Nothing fancy. Just some food and conversation."

"That would be perfect," Amanda answered cheerfully.

"Fabulous," Joyce exclaimed half-heartedly as she pulled a pen and a piece of paper from her purse. Using her car as a hard surface, she scribbled her address and she continued, "Come around five. We'll share a glass of wine. Or lemonade?" She glanced at Amanda with a mocking grin.

Amanda laughed and retorted, "I can handle wine once in a while. I'll even bring a bottle for dinner."

"Don't be silly. Don't bring anything. I'll take care of the food *and* wine." She handed Amanda the piece of paper and concluded, "So I'll see you at five?"

"I'll be there. Thank you very much for the invitation."

"You're most welcome."

Joyce drove away with a mix of emotions she couldn't explain. She was elated she'd get to see Amanda so soon, but frustrated it wouldn't be the kind of dinner she'd promised Amanda, the *tête-à-tête* she probably wanted even more than she could admit to herself.

She used the Bluetooth capabilities of her car to call Barbara. "It's happening tomorrow. Make sure you and Heather don't show up before six o'clock."

"Tomorrow? But Heather probably has plans for tomorrow by now…" Barbara started to protest.

"That's your problem. It's tomorrow or never." Joyce knew she wouldn't find the nerve to trick Amanda again.

CHAPTER SEVENTEEN

Amanda decided to walk to Joyce's. It was a little over a mile from her condo and she knew they'd drink some wine. She didn't feel comfortable driving after so much as a single sip of wine.

She'd never explored so far up Garland Street before. When she'd first turned onto the street, she was surprised Joyce could live in such an environment. Some of the older homes were clearly not being well taken care of. Several had broken windows and were in desperate need of paint. As she moved further up the hill, however, homes were newer, bigger, and built on larger lots with mature trees. There were definitely two distinctive worlds on Garland Street: down the hill and up the hill.

She slowed as she approached Joyce's home, though not because of the steep slope of the street. She'd left her condo much too soon. Not wanting to arrive ridiculously early, she kept looking at her watch and adjusting her pace as she admired the beautiful homes. She marveled at their size. She'd never wanted such a large house for herself, and she wondered how

Joyce could live in one of them alone with Dingo. It seemed like a lot of wasted space.

It was a hot August day and people were outside, mowing their lawns or taking in the late afternoon sun. Most smiled or nodded at her politely as she walked by. Others looked her over from head to toe as if suggesting someone dressed in denim shorts, a white tank top with a green sweater over it, and hiking boots didn't belong in this section of the street. She nervously closed a fist around the strap of her messenger bag, took a deep breath, and started ignoring everyone. She refused to be judged by these people. She'd dressed the way she always dressed, the only way she knew how and the only way she felt comfortable. Joyce was used to her fashion sense and didn't seem to mind it, and that was all that mattered.

Joyce. Amanda was looking forward to spending time alone with her again. She didn't know what they'd eat for dinner or what they'd talk about, but she knew she'd have a good time.

She was just five minutes early when she finally made it to the address Joyce had given her. She smiled at the sight of the home, a two-story house with sage green siding. It was secluded, set approximately one hundred feet from the street and almost entirely hidden behind large trees. Amanda had difficulty believing she was merely a mile from downtown Bangor.

She made her way to the front porch and rang the doorbell, her heart pounding at the thought of seeing Joyce. Her host quickly opened the door, looking as elegant as ever. She wore white Capri pants, a black camisole, and a silk scarf in shades of gray and pink. Amanda recognized the silver bracelet she'd worn before. Her makeup was light but enhanced her dark gray eyes. She was breathtakingly beautiful.

"You made it," Joyce said, looking for something over Amanda's shoulder. "Where's your car?"

"I walked."

"Up that hill? And not a drop of sweat," she added as she scrutinized Amanda's face. Amanda felt much warmer in that instant than she had walking "up that hill."

"It's not that bad."

"Not for you, of course," Joyce teased. "Well, come in. Welcome to Dingo's domain."

Amanda chuckled and followed Joyce inside. "Something smells delicious."

"It's the chicken grilling," Joyce explained as she walked to the kitchen, where she focused her attention on the boneless chicken breasts cooking in a non-stick grill pan on the stove. "I need to finish cooking the chicken so it can cool off a little before I finish our meal later. I'm making a summer salad with three kinds of lettuce, grilled chicken, watermelon, feta cheese, and cucumber. I hope you'll like it."

"I'm sure I will. It sounds yummy."

"Every time we've shared a meal together before we always ate fried food. I thought I'd cook something fresh and healthy for a change."

"Great idea. Can I do anything to help?"

"No, I already cut and prepared all the ingredients and they're waiting in the fridge. I just need to finish this chicken. I could have used the outside grill, but I haven't used that thing in three years because I'm scared to change the gas tank. It was Evelyn's toy."

"I could help you with that sometime."

Joyce turned to her long enough to offer a grateful smile and say, "Thank you," before she returned to her task.

Joyce was taking the fully cooked chicken off the stove when they heard Dingo yodel. Amanda thought the sound might have come from upstairs. "Where is he?" she inquired.

"He's up in my bedroom, in his crate. He usually sleeps on his bed in the living room when I'm home, but I figured he'd be too excited to see you and would want to follow us around."

"Oh, poor little guy. Can we go get him? I don't mind carrying him around if I need to."

Joyce scoffed a laugh. "What? You practically forced me to start using that evil crate and now you go soft on me with that 'poor little guy' stuff?"

"Oh, I still think the crate is a great idea. But not while I'm here." They both laughed and Joyce playfully hit Amanda's thigh with a dish towel that was sitting by the stove.

"All right, Miss Double Standards. Go get him while I put the chicken away and serve us some wine. First door on the left at the top of the stairs. He'll be happy to see you." Amanda smiled and started walking toward the stairs, her heart bouncing up and down with exhilaration. Spending time with Joyce in the privacy of her home felt so natural, so comfortable and, most of all, so enjoyable.

She walked upstairs and opened the door to Joyce's bedroom. It surprised her. She recognized her friend in the minimalist, uncluttered character of the home and the room, as well as in some of the artwork hanging on the walls. The traditional shades of brown and beige of the decor, however, didn't seem to fit with Joyce, the Creative Child. The outside grill was not the only thing that still remained of Evelyn, she decided. The decor had to be a result of her tastes, not Joyce's.

When she reached the crate, Dingo was standing up, his tail wagging furiously. He looked pitiful wearing his Elizabethan collar.

"Hi, there, little man. I see your mommy's been listening to the mean vet, huh? Poor you." She opened the door, removed the large plastic cone over his head, and took Dingo in her arms. The dog licked her cheek in appreciation. "Let's go eat some chicken, okay?"

When she got back to the kitchen with Dingo in her arms, Joyce was waiting for her with two glasses of wine. "Wait, I'll put him down. I don't think he'll run very far from me."

"Fine, you're the vet. I trust you know what you're doing." Joyce grinned. As soon as she put Dingo down, he lay by her feet and Joyce handed her a glass of wine. "It's pinot grigio. I hope you'll like it."

Amanda took a small sip and enjoyed its subtle sweetness. "Delicious," she confirmed, to her host's relief.

"Great. We'll go savor it on the patio, but first I'd like to show you something. Will you follow me?"

"Of course, we'll follow you." Amanda placed her glass on the counter and picked up Dingo again, ready to follow Joyce, who giggled as she watched Amanda's interaction with the basenji.

She followed her through French doors into the living room, where she spotted Dingo's bed. She took a peek at the patio and the magnificent view of the Penobscot River before reaching another set of French doors. When Amanda entered the smaller room beyond them, she gasped.

Although it was much smaller than any other room she'd seen so far, this room's pure white walls and the abundant light coming through a single large window made it look bigger. It was devoid of any furniture except for a small wooden table where paint and brushes sat and a large easel where an incomplete painting of Dingo waited. Other finished paintings were hung on the walls while others were simply sitting on the floor, leaning against one wall.

"So this is your room," she said, putting Dingo on the floor after she heard Joyce close the French doors behind them.

"My room? What do you mean?"

Amanda hesitated before she explained. She didn't want to offend Joyce, but it was too late to back out now. The words had escaped her mouth and betrayed her thoughts the minute she'd entered the only room in the house in which she recognized Joyce's essence. The Joyce she knew. "I mean, it seems to me like of all the rooms in this house, this room is the one that's really you. Am I wrong?"

Joyce smiled and sighed at the same time. "No. In fact, you're absolutely right." Her eyes glistened with tears even as she kept smiling. She seemed grateful Amanda had identified this particular space as hers. "It used to be Evelyn's office. I cleared everything out and painted the walls. Now it's my art studio. No one else has seen it yet. You're the first," she finished in almost a whisper.

Amanda instinctively understood the importance of Joyce's statement. She was showing her part of the essence she'd been working so hard to rediscover in the past several months. She was sharing her truth with her before anyone else. It was a privilege she wanted to honor. "Thank you for showing me. It's a beautiful space. And I love your art. You're a very talented Creative Child, you know."

"Oh no, I'm just playing. But it's important to me," Joyce said, leaning against the French doors. Amanda felt her watching her every move as she took a closer look at the paintings.

She didn't know anything about art, but she liked the simplicity of Joyce's watercolors on white background. Her art was almost childlike or cartoonish, yet some elements were surprisingly realistic. The color splatters added an element of surprise that made her style unique. As she went through the portraits of Dingo and a few other animals, she felt like she was discovering another part of Joyce, a part she'd chosen to share with no one else but her. The thought filled her heart with pride.

She laughed when she got to the painting of Dingo wearing his black bandage with a small red fire hydrant sticker, the first bandage she'd done for Dingo. "I painted that the first day we met at the clinic," Joyce explained as she moved closer to Amanda and looked over her shoulder.

Joyce's proximity mixed with the realization that their first meeting was somehow immortalized in that painting of Dingo gave Amanda chills. "I love it. I think it's my favorite."

"You should have it, then," Joyce whispered tenderly, her breath tickling the small hairs on the back of Amanda's neck, under her ponytail.

Amanda was sorely tempted to lean backward against Joyce, to have her take her in her arms in that intimate moment, but she managed to resist her impulse. "Oh no, Joyce, I didn't say that so you would give it to me. You've put so much work into it."

"If you love it, it's yours. Art is meant to be shared, you know. If anyone should have this painting, it's you. Please, take it. It would mean a lot to me for you to have it."

Amanda turned to Joyce and saw that she was sincere. "Okay, thank you very much."

"You're welcome." They held each other's gaze for a few seconds. As they did so, Amanda saw something she hadn't seen before in Joyce's eyes: an intensity that she found both seductive and enigmatic. Just as she thought Joyce might be leaning toward her, though, she suddenly straightened up and the mysterious expression in her eyes was instantly replaced with the joyful sparkle she was more familiar with. "Okay, ready for that wine now? We should go drink it on the patio so we can enjoy the view. Come on."

Amanda picked up Dingo and followed her almost regretfully. The art studio had exposed a part of Joyce she wanted to see again, bringing them to a new level of closeness she hoped could be duplicated outside of the room.

Joyce and Amanda sat quietly on two chaise lounges on the patio, admiring the view. Joyce was working on her second glass of pinot grigio while Amanda was still sipping on her first. Dingo lay on the patio between them. Joyce had thought she might have to place him in his dog pen, but he'd shown no desire to explore the yard yet, content to sleep between their chairs.

They'd talked about her art, Dingo, the kind of trees found on her property, the neighbors, everything and anything. There had been comfortable silences they hadn't felt compelled to fill, allowing themselves to get lost in the view of the river. Like Dingo, Joyce was content. Or almost.

She kept glancing at her watch, hoping Barbara hadn't been able to convince Heather that dinner with her aunt might be more fun than any plans she'd already made for this Saturday night. She was enjoying Amanda's visit even more than she'd thought and she wanted it to go on forever. Just the two of them. And Dingo, of course.

Then again, if she remained alone with Amanda, she might be tempted to kiss her, as she'd been tempted earlier in her art studio. Sharing her special room with Amanda, inviting her in, had been akin to inviting her into her soul—and she'd fitted perfectly there, in her space and in her heart. In that moment, she'd wanted to get even closer. She'd managed to stop herself from kissing Amanda then, but she didn't know if she could find the strength to do it again.

It was becoming all too clear to her that her feelings for Amanda went beyond friendship. She had to put that attraction back where it belonged, hidden deep inside her, before she got hurt or before she put Amanda in an awkward position. Amanda deserved to find love with a nice woman her own age. She didn't deserve the unwanted advances of a woman old enough to be her mother. Joyce had to find a way to stay away from moments like the one they'd shared in her art studio.

By six thirty Joyce thought Barbara and Heather might not show up, and she was getting hungry. "I should go inside to finish the salad," she told Amanda. "Do you want another glass of wine?"

"No, thank you, but I'll come in with you to help."

Before they could move from their seats, Joyce heard the sliding door open and she cringed in anticipation. "There you are," she heard her sister say. "We rang the doorbell, but when there was no answer I figured you might be back here."

Joyce heard Amanda gasp with surprise and saw her straighten up in her seat, instantaneously nervous. She swallowed, took a deep breath, and stood up. It was too late to change her mind. Now was the time to play her part.

"Barbara? What are you doing here?"

Heather followed Barbara through the sliding door. She was wearing tight jeans and a blue tank top that showed off her perfectly perky thirty-year-old breasts. Blond hair flowed freely below her shoulders. Tan skin and light blue eyes completed her heartbreaker looks. "Mom said you invited us for dinner. Oh, I see you already have company."

Joyce recognized the smile Heather sent Amanda's way as soon as she noticed her. Barbara was right. All it took for a woman to become Heather's prey was to be attractive, and Amanda more than met that condition. "I did invite you for dinner. Tomorrow."

"Mom?" Heather questioned her mother.

"Tomorrow? Are you sure?" Barbara said as she grabbed her cell phone and checked her calendar to confirm, exactly as she'd said she would when she'd shared the details of her plan with Joyce. "Oh my god, you're right," she continued as she turned her phone toward Heather. She was playing her role perfectly.

"For Christ's sake, Mom," Heather said with less exasperation than Joyce had expected, most likely because of Amanda's presence.

"I'm so sorry. I was sure it was today. We can go and come back tomorrow if you want," Barbara went on.

"Don't be silly. There's more than enough for four," Joyce offered, hoping her answer didn't sound too wooden.

"I can go," Amanda chimed in timidly as she rose from her chaise lounge.

"Absolutely not," Joyce protested before she physically stopped Amanda by briefly catching her hand. "No one's going anywhere." She smiled at Amanda, hoping to relieve some of the panic she saw in her face.

Amanda's smile was hesitant, but when she finally expressed her agreement with a subtle nod, Joyce proceeded to make introductions. "Amanda, this is my sister, Barbara, and my niece, Heather. Ladies, this is Amanda, Dingo's vet and my dear friend."

"Nice to meet you, Amanda," Barbara said as the three women shook hands properly. The game officially started and it was leaving Joyce's stomach in knots. Heather started to chat with Amanda and Joyce realized that Barbara's little scenario was unfolding exactly as she'd planned. Amanda obviously had sparked her niece's interest.

Amanda, however, didn't seem to share her enthusiasm. The arrival of two women she didn't know seemed to have made her extremely nervous. Joyce had expected that that would be the case. She'd even expected that she'd feel guilty for making her social anxiety flair up. She had not been prepared for her own physical reaction to causing Amanda such distress. She felt nauseous, disgusted with herself. She deeply regretted her part in her sister's scheme now, but there didn't seem to be any other choice than to go through with it. "Well, I'll go inside and finish the salad," she announced. "Barbara, will you help me?"

"I'll help," Amanda offered, following Joyce.

"We'll all help," Heather added, refusing to let her quarry get away so easily.

"Great," Joyce agreed.

She let the two younger women inside first and resisted the urge to vomit when Barbara proudly winked at her. She turned away and started to walk in, but Barbara held her back with a hand. "Are we really having salad? Just salad?"

Joyce didn't try to hide her frustration when she sighed, especially since Amanda and Heather were already in the kitchen and couldn't hear her. "Yes, we're having salad. If you'd come tomorrow, you might have gotten filet mignon. But today, we're having salad." She then childishly stuck her tongue out at her sister, which didn't make her feel better.

* * *

"I brought dessert," Barbara announced. She stood up from the table and walked to the kitchen.

"I'll go make the coffee," Joyce added before she joined her sister. Amanda made a move to follow her, but Heather immediately asked her another question about her work at the clinic and she was forced to stay behind to answer.

The two of them had sat directly across from one another, and Heather had monopolized Amanda's attention during the entire dinner. Joyce knew that was the point of the evening, but she also couldn't help but notice Amanda didn't appear to be as comfortable as she'd been when she was alone with her. She'd been tempted to reach out and place her hand on Amanda's arm to comfort her several times, but held off after deciding that there had been no sign of the kind of severe anxiety that Amanda had experienced at the fair and the casino.

There was definitely some discomfort in her body language, however, and in the brief, polite responses she made to Heather's endless questions. She did answer her, though, and she even laughed nervously at some of Heather's jokes, which Joyce interpreted as some budding interest on Amanda's part. Heather's charms would take longer to work on Amanda, but they might succeed in the end.

"It's going wonderfully well, don't you think?" Barbara whispered to Joyce with Machiavellian pride once they were alone in the kitchen.

"I guess so, but Amanda isn't really herself with Heather yet. She can't relax," Joyce answered as she scooped coffee beans into her fancy Swiss coffee machine.

"Heather will find a way to make her relax, don't worry," Barbara added as she placed pieces of cheesecake on white plates. "I really like that girl, by the way. She seems smart and down-to-earth. I'm so excited about this, Joy. Thank you for making this happen." Barbara left the kitchen with two plated desserts, satisfaction showing in her bouncing steps.

"Yeah, I like her too," Joyce mumbled to herself with a sigh before she grabbed the cream and sugar and followed her sister to the dining room.

* * *

Amanda sat sideways on a chaise lounge and was preparing to stretch her legs and get comfortable when Heather hurried to sit right next to her on the same chair, pressing her arm and thigh into hers. Her proximity made Amanda nervous, but not in the pleasant way Joyce's had before. At the fair, on their walk by the stream, at the casino, and especially earlier in her art studio. She didn't enjoy being this close to Heather, but she didn't want to offend her, so she stayed put.

She'd accepted Heather's invitation for a walk after dinner for the same reason she was now sitting so close to her. She wanted to be polite. Heather had been extremely nice from the moment they'd met and she was certainly attractive, but the truth was that Amanda would have preferred staying behind and doing dishes with Joyce. She was here for Joyce, not for Heather or anyone else.

The evening that had started in such a perfect way and held so much promise was ending quite differently from what she'd imagined. She'd hoped for more closeness, more intimacy with Joyce. Instead she was sitting on a chaise lounge without Joyce, her side pressed to another woman's body. Frustrated with the turn of events, she reminded herself that there would be more dinners with Joyce. Alone with Joyce.

In the meantime, spending time with Heather was not that bad. She was making things easy for her. She directed the conversation, made her laugh, and didn't seem to mind her quiet nature. Amanda saw a lot of Joyce in her. She figured they could even become friends eventually.

"So, do you think you're in Bangor to stay?"

Since she'd sat together with her on the chaise lounge, Heather's voice had become lower, softer, and she was leaning toward Amanda every time she spoke.

"Yes, I do. I love it here. And your aunt has been very good to me."

"That's great. I sure would like for you to stay. And I'm glad my aunt has a friend like you. She's been so lonely since Evelyn's death. You know, the love those two shared was so strong. Aunt Joyce was lost without her Evelyn. Their love was the kind of love you're lucky to find once in a lifetime. It's so rare, so precious. I hope I find it someday."

"Yeah, me too," Amanda answered, lost in thoughts of Joyce and Evelyn. Was she really naive to hope Joyce could love again and that she could be the fortunate woman she would love? How could she compete with the kind of love Heather was describing? She swallowed with difficulty, feeling inadequate.

"I don't doubt you will, Amanda. You deserve the best, you know."

"Thank you," Amanda whispered, feeling her cheeks heat up with a blush.

"I mean it," Heather added in a breath. Amanda watched Heather's gaze move to her lips and she understood that her intentions went far beyond friendship.

Quickly, Amanda went over the evening in her mind, from the moment Heather and Barbara had arrived until now. She thought about Heather's multiple questions, her charming conversation, her invitation for a stroll on Joyce's property. Heather was hitting on her. Heavily. She'd always been dense about these things, oblivious to any attempt at seduction, but even she could see it now. As clear as day.

Heather's face moved closer to hers and she felt the blonde's breath on her cheek when she declared, "I'm glad my mother and my aunt arranged this dinner for us to meet." Heather's smile was languorous, her eyes half-closed.

"What?" was all Amanda could manage to say. She was barely starting to understand that Heather was trying to seduce her. Why were Joyce and her sister being added to the equation?

Heather chuckled before she answered. "You don't know them like I do, but let's say this wouldn't be their first brilliant scheme. I don't believe for one second this dinner was an accident," she explained. "My mother has always disapproved of my girlfriends. She's always wanted me to meet someone more intelligent, more driven, more…like you." She smiled again, even more seductively this time. "I'm starting to believe she was right."

"Wait," Amanda said. She stood up. She needed to put some distance between her and Heather. This was not a romantic moment. This was the most confusing situation she'd experienced in her lifetime and she needed to make sense of it. "You're saying that Joyce and your mother arranged this whole thing? That this evening was all a ploy for the two of us to meet?"

"Well, yes, but I'm not complaining about it." Heather stood and moved to get closer to Amanda. She grabbed her hands, but Amanda abruptly pulled them away. She backed away from Heather slowly and closed a fist around the leather strap of her messenger bag, tears rapidly filling her eyes. She didn't want to believe Joyce had done this to her, had used her, had tricked her as Heather was suggesting. Yet it made too much sense not to believe it. When Heather made another move toward her, she turned and ran.

She didn't stop running until she'd made her way down the hill, away from Joyce and her kind. When she reached the less affluent part of Garland Street, she slowed to a walk and started sobbing before she could catch her breath. Doug had been right to warn her against Joyce. She'd used their friendship as bait to offer her to Heather in a neatly wrapped package. She'd been tricked, played, deceived. She was disgusted with Joyce but even more with her own gullibility. She kept crying until she arrived at her condo, bawling so violently that she barely made it to her bathroom before she got sick.

* * *

Joyce and Barbara sat in the living room on the cream leather sofas, drinking another glass of wine while Dingo lay quietly on his dog bed. He whimpered when the sliding door opened and Heather came inside alone. She slumped next to Barbara on the sofa, defeated. "Where's Amanda?" Joyce asked with concern, turning to the sliding door that Heather had closed behind her.

"She left."

"What do you mean, she left?" Joyce asked sternly. She stood up and hurried to the front door but when she opened it she saw no sign of Amanda. She went back to the living room for an explanation, panicked, and heard her sister ask the questions she desperately wanted answers to.

"What happened? I thought the two of you were hitting it off."

"You really have no clue, do you, Mom?" Heather answered with the arrogance she'd kept in check all evening long for Amanda's sake.

"Why don't you explain it to me then?"

Joyce took Dingo in her arms before she sat back in the sofa facing Barbara and Heather, ready to listen. She needed Dingo to comfort her as much as she needed to comfort him.

Heather sighed with annoyance and rolled her eyes before she finally started to talk. "I tried, Mom. I really tried, despite the fact that you schemed behind my back to arrange this meeting."

"What on earth are you talking about?" Barbara protested.

"Don't you deny it! I know you, remember? You planned this whole thing and that's fucked up, but I tried anyway because okay, yeah, Amanda is super interesting. And she's totally hot in a geeky kind of way."

"You keep saying that you tried. What does that mean? You always get any girl you want. What happened?" Barbara questioned, abandoning her act on the spot.

"She's not interested in me, Mom. It's obvious."

"Is that why she left? Did you get too forward with her? Did you scare her away?"

"No. I don't think so."

A chill passed through Joyce as she figured out why Amanda might have run away. She had to know for sure. "Heather, did you tell Amanda you thought your mother and I arranged this dinner?"

"Well, yes," Heather admitted.

"Oh my god," Joyce said weakly before she closed her eyes. "She's going to hate me forever now." She was paralyzed with an overwhelming sensation of loss. She'd lost Amanda. She'd warned Joyce she didn't play games and wouldn't tolerate for her to play games with her either. It couldn't have been clearer. She'd betrayed her and she'd lost her. And she only had herself to blame.

"I don't think she'll hate you, Aunt Joyce," Heather mumbled with spite, her arms crossed over her chest.

"What do you mean?" Barbara asked. "For god's sake, child, it's like pulling teeth. Enough already. You're going to sit up straight and tell me and your aunt everything. You hear me?"

Heather reluctantly straightened up on the sofa and looked directly into Joyce's eyes when she spoke. Joyce tightened her hold on Dingo, bracing herself to listen. "We went for a walk and it was very nice, but she didn't bite. None of my moves, looks, smiles, nothing seemed to work. When I told her I was glad the both of you arranged for us to meet, she freaked out and she left."

"Why didn't she bite?" Barbara probed.

Heather laughed. "Oh my god, are you two really that clueless? Amanda's not into me, Mom. She's into Aunt Joyce."

"What?" Joyce asked in a low, barely audible voice.

"Didn't you two see how hard I had to work to keep her attention all through dinner? She always turned to Aunt Joyce before she answered my questions. I even had to keep her from following her to the kitchen. I mean, I had a feeling I was spinning my wheels then, but the way she reacted when I told her I thought you'd planned the whole thing confirmed my suspicions. If she'd been into me at all, she'd have laughed the whole thing off. But the way she ran from here…"

"What, Heather? Did she say anything?" Joyce's voice cracked and her eyes welled up with tears. Her heart tightened in her chest.

"No. She didn't say anything. But it was obvious she was heartbroken."

Joyce squeezed Dingo against her heart and didn't try to stop her tears.

"That makes no sense," Barbara argued vehemently. "Your aunt is old enough to be her mother. Why are you making this shit up?"

"I'm not making anything up. The heart wants what the heart wants. Now if you'll excuse me, I think I'll go and meet my friends in town."

"I came with you, Heather, can't you wait?"

"No. I've wasted enough of this night, thanks to you. Now you come with me and I'll drop you off, or you stay here. It's up to you."

"Go," Joyce said before Barbara could decide. "I'll be okay. Actually, I need to be alone."

"Fine. If you say so."

Joyce placed Dingo back in his dog bed and walked her sister and goddaughter to the door. She felt numb. Barbara gave her air kisses. "It's better this way, Baby Sis. If Heather's right Amanda would have gotten her heart broken sooner or later anyway. It's not like the two of you could actually have a relationship, right? Can you imagine?"

"Right," Joyce simply said, finding no energy to protest the manner her sister had chosen to comfort her.

To Joyce's surprise, Heather hugged her tight and whispered into her ear, "Amanda's a catch and you deserve a second chance at love. Don't listen to Mother." She kissed Joyce's cheek and left the house, followed by her mother.

CHAPTER EIGHTEEN

Amanda's eyes were still puffy when she went back to the clinic on Monday morning. She'd cried until she'd fallen asleep from exhaustion on Saturday and woke up on Sunday only to cry some more. Joyce called and texted her a few times begging for a few minutes to talk to her, but she ignored every call and every text message. She knew that if Joyce had been able to play with her mind before, she could easily do it again. The safest thing to do was to stay away from her.

Amanda had hoped the walk to the clinic would ease her eyes, her brains, her heart, everything, but all it achieved was to give her time to figure out how she might avoid questions from her coworkers, especially from Doug, once she got to work. The best strategy she'd come up with was to avoid them all and keep to herself even more than usual.

The clinic was busy that day, for which Amanda was extremely grateful. A full schedule provided distraction from her broken heart and doubled as the perfect way to hide from concerned coworkers. Doug had to cancel the usual Monday morning staff meeting, and Amanda didn't have time to stop and have lunch in the break room, where she might have been forced to answer a few questions. Destiny seemed to be on her side.

She'd made it through most of the day before she had to tell a young couple that Winston, their Lhasa Apso companion, was suffering from serious heart disease. When she explained that medication would allow their nine-year-old dog to live another twelve to eighteen months before inevitable heart failure, the couple held on to each other in a desperate embrace while they cried their eyes out. She remained strong for the young couple, comforting them as she was trained to do in such situations.

As soon as Winston left with his owners, however, she ran to the restroom where she broke down into tears. Someone else entered and left the unisex restroom during the twenty minutes she spent locked in a stall, and she hoped that whoever it was didn't hear her crying. More than anything she hoped it wasn't Doug. She could brush off anyone else's inquiries, but she feared she couldn't do the same with him.

Her worst nightmare came true when she came out of the restroom and saw him leaning against the wall right next to the restroom door. "Can I see you in my office for a minute?" he asked softly.

"I still have to see Mrs. Johnson's cat."

"It can wait. I just need a minute."

Amanda sighed with resignation and followed him to his office. He closed the door behind them. "You have two options, Amanda. You tell me what's going on right now, or you're coming over for dinner tonight so Susan can get it out of you. What will it be?"

"There's nothing wrong. I'm just tired."

"Wrong answer, partner. I heard you crying in there."

Amanda sighed again. She didn't have the strength to have dinner with Doug and his family that night and she knew he wouldn't let it go. She decided to come clean. "You were right about Joyce Allen. I should have listened to you."

"Oh Amanda, I'm so sorry. Did she hurt you?"

Amanda nodded her answer and felt her face contort in a desperate attempt to hold her tears. Despite all of her efforts, she started sobbing and did something she could never have imagined in any circumstance. She moved closer to Doug, placed her head and hands against his chest and cried into his scrubs. Doug only hesitated for a second or two before he put his arms around her and held her. He didn't stroke her hair or her back as she assumed someone like Joyce would do, but his strong arms were enough to soothe her. Doug might lack finesse but his embrace was honest.

When she stopped crying and moved away from Doug he reached out for a box of tissues on his desk and handed one to her. She blew her nose and he cleared his throat. "Is Joyce Allen coming back with her dog for another bandage?"

"Not before next Friday."

"Good. I'll take the appointment. You need to stay away from that woman. I don't know what she did to you, but I know she'll do it again."

"I can do my job. You don't have to protect me."

"I don't have to, but I want to. It's no big deal. We'll switch appointments that day and any other day she needs to be here with her dog. Okay?"

"Okay," Amanda agreed weakly.

After a moment of hesitation, Doug placed his hands on her upper arms and squeezed lightly. "And don't forget I'm here if you need to talk."

"Okay," she said again. An awkward silence followed; it was clear Doug didn't know what else he was supposed to do. She pushed her glasses up the bridge of her nose with her finger and squared her shoulders. "Well, I better get to Mrs. Johnson's cat."

"Oh right, yes, of course." He stepped aside so she could get to the door.

She put her hand on the door handle and without turning around she said, "Thank you, Doug." She left his office before he had time to acknowledge her gratitude.

CHAPTER NINETEEN

Joyce sat in the waiting room of the Perry Veterinary Clinic with Dingo on her lap and the painting she'd given Amanda on the chair next to her. She'd run so fast she'd left it behind. Joyce doubted she wanted it anymore, but she'd brought it nonetheless. She hoped it would remind Amanda of what they'd shared that evening before Barbara and Heather had showed up and ruined everything.

She corrected herself. Before *she* had ruined everything. She could have said no to Barbara. She should have said no. She'd actually meant to say no, until she'd thought Amanda was ready to meet someone and that introducing her to Heather could help.

She'd never thought in a million years that Amanda could be interested in her. Not with the twenty-four years that separated them. She'd replayed the conversation they'd had at the casino over and over in her mind after hearing Heather say that the only person Amanda was interested in was Joyce. When Amanda had revealed that she'd never believed she could find love before she'd met Joyce, she'd assumed that hearing about her relationship with Evelyn had led the young woman to open up to love, but that was not what Amanda meant at all. As shy as she was, she couldn't have been clearer that day. She was opening up to the possibility of love because of Joyce. Not because of Joyce and Evelyn, but because of Joyce alone.

Joyce had barely slept since Amanda had run from her house two weeks ago. She didn't know if or how a relationship with Amanda could be possible. All she knew, all she obsessed about, was that she needed to talk to her, to spend time with her again. If she could only convince Amanda to forgive her, they could figure out the rest together. She saw this visit to the clinic as her last chance to explain herself or at least to persuade Amanda to meet with her so they could talk about what had happened.

A young man approached her in the waiting room. "The doctor will see you now, Ms. Allen."

"Oh, okay." Surprised not to see Isabelle, Joyce grabbed the painting in one hand and with her other hand used the lead to guide Dingo. He was doing well enough to handle a short walk. They followed the young man to a different exam room, which surprised Joyce again. Something was definitely off. She let go of the painting only long enough to place Dingo on the exam table and then held the framed art nervously against her chest.

When she saw Doug Perry enter the exam room, she gasped. Amanda was obviously avoiding her at all costs, but she couldn't give up. She simply couldn't. "Where is Doctor Carter?"

"She's not available. I'll take care of Dingo today. Let's see that leg," Doctor Perry explained coldly without even looking at her.

Dingo growled when the veterinarian put his hands on him. No, this would not work. For Dingo or for her.

"If Doctor Carter can't see us now we'll wait. She's been Dingo's vet through his entire recovery and she promised she'd take care of him until he's fully recovered."

"Ms. Allen, Doctor Carter is not available and I can take care of Dingo as well as she can. Matt, will you help me?" His tone was barely polite.

"No!" she said louder. "I'm sorry, Doctor Perry, but that won't do. I demand to see Doctor Carter." She hadn't heard that tone in her voice in so long that she was shocked to find it was still in her. It was a tone she'd always hated, one she'd used in her former life, when she and Evelyn got poor service in stores or restaurant. Demanding to see the manager had almost been a hobby back then. She didn't miss that now, but she didn't want to go through this visit with Doctor Perry. She wasn't acting like a spoiled rich girl who wasn't getting what she wanted; she was acting out of sheer despair.

"You're in no position to demand anything here, Ms. Allen."

"Excuse me?"

"You heard me."

She held his gaze, but she didn't know how long she could keep her defiant attitude when all she wanted to do was to fall to her knees and cry. She heard the door open but didn't look away from him before she heard Amanda's voice. "I'll see Dingo, Doug. It's okay."

"Are you sure?"

"Yes. I could hear you and Ms. Allen all the way to my office and we certainly don't want to disturb our clients and patients, do we? So I'll take care of Dingo."

"Okay, but I won't be far if you need me."

"Thank you."

Doug Perry and the young male vet tech left the exam room, but Joyce couldn't claim she'd won the battle. She'd managed to get Amanda to examine Dingo but her attitude was glacial and she was avoiding any eye contact. She focused all of her attention to Dingo's leg, conducting her exam without saying a word. Joyce wanted to cry even more now that she was faced with Amanda's hostility, now that she could almost touch it.

"I brought the painting I gave you. You forgot it the other night." She risked placing the portrait of Dingo next to its subject on the exam table, where Amanda would be forced to see it.

"You can take it back with you. I don't want it anymore. I'll take Dingo to the back with me and we'll change his bandage. You know where the waiting room is."

"But I wanted to watch, like the other times."

"That won't be possible. Not today, Ms. Allen."

Joyce watched as Amanda took Dingo into her arms and left the room. How could she convince Amanda to talk to her when she couldn't even get the woman to look at her? If only Amanda had seen her face. She would have been forced then to recognize her distress. She grabbed the painting and took it back to the waiting room, the harsh reality of the situation beginning to register. She'd lost Amanda.

"That's a good boy," Amanda said as soothingly as she could while she removed Dingo's bandage. Isabelle was holding him on his side on the table. He was more nervous than he'd been every time they'd replaced his bandage before. She wasn't surprised. He was simply reacting to her own anxiety.

Being in the same room with Joyce had brought her pain back to the unbearable level it had been when she'd run down Garland Street. Doug was right. She was too fragile to be in Joyce's presence. She couldn't even look at her for fear of completely losing it.

She hadn't been able to resist taking a peek at the painting she'd given her that night, however, and it had awakened something different in her. The past two weeks had been all about the torment and suffering caused by Joyce's mind games and betrayal. In clashing contrast, the painting had brought her back to Joyce's art studio, to a moment of intimacy she'd cherished. The portrait gnawed at her, trying to convince her that the closeness they'd shared before that damned dinner couldn't possibly have been nothing more than a game. She closed her eyes and sighed heavily. As much as she wanted to hold on to that hope, she couldn't risk it.

"Ms. Allen, Dingo's ready now, if you want to follow me," Isabelle said in the same friendly tone she always used. Joyce looked at her and wondered if she was oblivious to what was happening. Surely, she had to know she was in the presence of a woman who'd suffered a great loss. A woman who felt utterly and hopelessly empty. "Ms. Allen?"

"Yes, I'll follow you." No. She didn't know anything. How could she? No one could know how the brief friendship she'd shared with Amanda had changed her. She didn't really know it herself before she'd lost her.

Joyce entered the exam room and, holding the painting against her chest, kept staring at the door where Amanda would appear with Dingo. She looked at Joyce when she entered this time. She even smiled after she put Dingo down on the exam table, but there was no depth behind that smile. It was a polite smile that announced the professional behavior Joyce had demanded. You can't demand friendship, caring, or forgiveness, Joyce reminded herself. She didn't smile back. Instead, she felt tears run down her cheeks.

"So, no more splint for Dingo, as we'd planned. We made this soft bandage out of cotton wadding and elastic tape. He needs to keep it on for two weeks. You can let him walk longer now, even run a little, but no jumping yet. Do you have any questions?"

Joyce shook her head and placed the painting on the exam table so she could move Dingo to the floor and clip his leash to his collar. "Antibiotics?" she managed to say as she fought to keep her quiet tears from turning to sobs.

"Yes, Isabelle is getting them ready and is probably waiting for you at the reception desk."

Joyce nodded and reached for the painting. "I'll keep it, if you still want me to have it," Amanda said.

Joyce smiled weakly. "I do."

"Okay, good. Thank you."

"I'm so sorry, Amanda. I never meant to hurt you." Joyce wanted to reach out and pull Amanda into her arms, but she rushed to open the door for her and wouldn't meet her gaze again. Joyce left without another word. There was no fight left in her.

CHAPTER TWENTY

"I'm not in the mood to go out and meet Heather's new girlfriend, Barb. I'm not going to act happy just because you want me to. I miss her. She was the best thing that happened to me in years and I fucking miss her. I can't help it. I should never have gone ahead with your plan."

Joyce placed a glass of white wine on the breakfast bar in front of Barbara and waited for her reaction. Barbara had stopped by on her way to the restaurant where she was to meet Heather and her new conquest. She'd asked Joyce to join them, but it was out of the question. She was already in her pajamas and ready to wallow in misery.

A week had passed since she'd seen Amanda at the clinic and Joyce still couldn't get the visit out of her mind. She couldn't help but wonder if she should have tried harder. Amanda's cold detachment had paralyzed her and she'd been unable to beg for forgiveness the way she'd prepared to do. Part of her was resigned to the fact that she'd lost Amanda, but another part, the part that missed her so much it ached, wasn't convinced.

"Ridiculous," Barbara responded before she took a large gulp of her wine.

"What?"

"This whole thing is completely ridiculous. I mean listen to yourself. So you had a crush on a girl young enough to be your daughter. And she probably had a thing for you too. But so what? It's not like it could've worked out anyway, is it? I mean, can you imagine?"

"Fuck you, Barb."

"Oh, that's mature. Well done, Joy."

"Fuck you. I mean it. I can't deal with you right now. Go meet your daughter now so I can cuddle with my dog, will you?"

"Are you kicking me out?"

"Yes, I am."

Barbara held her gaze for a few seconds before she started laughing. "How much wine have you had already?"

"Too much." Joyce had opened the bottle and started to drink before Barbara's arrival, hoping to relax. She'd emptied the bottle in Barbara's clean glass.

"All right, you're off the hook because I understand wine can make us say things we don't mean, but I'll get out of here before you get any nastier."

"At last," Joyce said bluntly, slightly frustrated when Barbara laughed harder.

She followed her sister to the door and they shared air kisses. "Now go on and cuddle with your sack of germs. No more wine for you, okay?"

"Whatever."

Barbara smiled at her and sounded almost motherly when she added, "You will get over it, I promise. And you'll see it was better this way."

Barbara left and closed the door behind her. "Fuck you," Joyce said again. She picked up Dingo and brought him upstairs with her. "You're sleeping with me tonight. I love your germs."

She climbed upstairs and got into bed with Dingo, who didn't argue with her, quickly settling between her arm and the side of her body as she plunged her fingers into his red fur.

Joyce went over Barbara's words and soon her mind was filled with the same series of questions she'd asked herself a thousand times since she'd found out Amanda might be interested in her. Was the way things ended truly preferable to attempting a relationship with the younger woman? Why was their age difference so important to her?

On one hand, did she think a relationship with Amanda would be inappropriate because of her own convictions or because she knew Evelyn and Barbara wouldn't approve? On the other hand, if she did develop a relationship with Amanda, would it be simply to go against Evelyn's and Barbara's rules of conduct?

Of course, there was no way to find out unless she tried, and she'd missed that opportunity, hadn't she? "Damn it, little brat, I screwed everything up, didn't I?"

Joyce stared into Dingo's eyes until he succumbed to sleep. She kept petting him, the movement of her hand and the softness of his fur soothing her. She was about to doze off when a thought flashed through her wine-clouded mind. Amanda had kept Dingo's portrait in the end, hadn't she? If she truly had wanted nothing to do with Joyce, she wouldn't have accepted the gift. After all, it wasn't only an image of Dingo. It was a picture Joyce had painted. There was hope, she thought as her eyelids got heavier. There was an opening, and she'd be a fool not to try to stick her foot in it before it closed again.

She reached out to the bedside table with her free hand and grabbed her cell phone. She typed up her message to Amanda before she could change her mind again. Or before she sobered up.

"Need to explain. Please. Tomorrow?"

She stared at the phone until its display screen got dark, then she dropped it to her stomach. She was still waiting for a reply when sleep claimed her.

Amanda was resting in bed when she heard the notification of an incoming text message. She'd been staring at the painting on her dark wood, six-drawer dresser. She hadn't decided where or if she'd hang the portrait of Dingo yet, but she spent time admiring it every night. It wasn't as painful as she'd expected at first.

While the thoughts of Joyce that flashed through her mind during the day were still gloomy and painful, the painting brought up different, more comforting ones. When she looked at it she allowed herself to remember the Joyce she'd seen as a birthday present from the universe. She focused on Joyce's *joie de vivre*, her determination, her laughter. She drew a mental picture of her thick silver hair, her dark gray, laughing eyes, and her inviting, often playful smile.

She reached out to grab her phone from the bedside table and was surprised when she saw Joyce's name on the display screen. Joyce hadn't sent her another text message since she'd left the clinic after her last visit. Amanda thought she'd given up, which strangely both relieved her and saddened her. She read Joyce's message a few times and sighed with frustration.

Doug's voice got louder and louder in her mind, telling her she'd be an idiot to respond. That she needed to stay away from Joyce and her mind games. She should delete the message right away and block Joyce's number once and for all.

Her own voice, however, as small and hesitant as it was, couldn't be ignored. She wanted to hear Joyce's explanation. She wanted to find out if there was any way to reconcile the woman she remembered every time she looked at the portrait of Dingo with the woman who'd lured her to her house for her niece. There had to be a middle ground between the perfection she'd seen in Joyce and the pure evil Doug saw in her.

Amanda sat on her bed and typed her answer with trembling thumbs. "Meet me in front of my building, nine a.m. We'll take a walk."

CHAPTER TWENTY-ONE

Joyce was standing by the door of Amanda's building at eight fifty-five. She'd been so happy to see Amanda's reply to her text message when she'd opened her eyes that morning *sans* headache, amazingly enough. Her relief and enthusiasm had followed her through her morning routine: going outside with Dingo, feeding him and herself, taking a shower, doing her hair and makeup, and getting dressed. She'd even caught herself whistling a few times. As soon as she got in her car and started driving toward Franklin Street, however, a deep fear took root inside her. There was a great possibility, after all, that her explanation wouldn't suffice. Amanda had generously granted her this meeting, but that didn't in any way guarantee she would earn her forgiveness.

Joyce paced on the sidewalk, waiting for Amanda. She pulled on the slightly heavier and larger scarf she'd chosen to wear. She'd dressed for the chilly early September morning with jeans and a light knit sweater, but she hoped the day wouldn't warm up too quickly. Loosening her scarf, revealing the unmistakable signs of aging it concealed—that would surely scare Amanda away for good.

Amanda showed up in her usual layered look and ponytail. She pushed her glasses up the bridge of her nose in a familiar movement Joyce found endearing. Her smile was hesitant. Joyce answered it without restraint. Amanda had every right to be cautious. "Thank you so much for meeting me."

Amanda jerked her chin toward the walking trail. "Let's walk."

They walked side by side in silence for a few minutes. Joyce had hoped Amanda would open the conversation, ask her questions, but it soon became evident she was there to listen to Joyce's plea and nothing else. Joyce had gone over and over what she might say if she had the chance to, but she'd never worked on an opening statement. Where to begin? She pulled on her scarf, cleared her throat, and the first words that came out surprised her. "I miss you." The tears that followed shocked her even more.

Amanda glanced at Joyce and stopped walking. She sighed with frustration and looked up to the sky. Joyce couldn't decide if she was annoyed with her for crying or with the tears rapidly filling her own eyes. She took tissues out of her messenger bag and handed a few to Joyce.

"Thank you."

"I thought you wanted to talk to me. So talk, please. I've done enough crying already. Tell me why you invited me to your house without telling me your sister and niece would be there. Without telling me the objective of the evening was for me and Heather to hit it off. Why you tricked me that way after I told you how much I hated social and mind games and wouldn't tolerate them. Just tell me, please."

So there it was. The opening Joyce had been waiting for. Amanda started crying harder after delivering it, but when Joyce made a move toward her to comfort her, she took a step back and raised her hand in front of her. "Just talk," she repeated as she started walking again.

"I didn't want to do it, Amanda," Joyce started. "It was Barbara's idea."

"Are you going to tell me she forced you?" Amanda scoffed, irritated.

"No, of course not. Please let me finish. I'm taking full responsibility for what happened, but I have to start from the beginning. Okay?"

Amanda nodded and lowered her gaze to the ground in front of her as they walked. Joyce focused on the stream to the right of the walking trail and continued, "You see, my sister has never approved of Heather's girlfriends. She thinks they're not driven enough and have no real substance. I can't say she's wrong, to be honest. So when I told Barbara about you, Dingo's veterinarian and my new, young lesbian friend, she immediately asked me to introduce you to Heather. She thought you'd be the perfect girlfriend for her daughter. I told my sister I would think about it, but I had no intentions of doing it. I didn't want to trick you like that. I didn't want to risk Heather hurting you. And, quite frankly, I didn't want to share you with anyone."

Joyce paused and glanced at Amanda, who didn't react otherwise to Joyce's revelation but slowed her step. Joyce matched her new pace and turned her attention back to the stream. "You're very important to me, Amanda. I loved the time we spent together and I didn't want you to spend that time with Heather. Or anyone else." She heard her take a deep breath. "But then at the casino you mentioned you might be ready to find someone to love and I thought perhaps I was being selfish. I thought if I did introduce you to Heather, you could find love with her or with one of her friends. I really meant well. I realize now that it wasn't a good reason to trick you into meeting Heather. I'm so sorry I did that, and I wish I could take it back."

They walked in silence for a few seconds before Amanda asked "Is that it?"

"Not really. But that covers why I planned that dinner, yes."

Amanda sighed again, but this time with less frustration. She seemed more relaxed. She stopped walking and turned to Joyce, who met her gaze. "If you'd told me what you were planning, I would've told you I wasn't interested in meeting anyone. None of this would've happened. You can't plan my love life behind my back, do you realize that?"

"I do, I so completely do. And I can't apologize enough for what I did."

"Good. Because if we're going to try to be friends again, there can't be any secrets between us."

"I know. That's why this conversation can't end here. If you really do want us to see each other again, there's something else we need to talk about, isn't there?"

"What do you mean?" Amanda looked to the ground, a blush coloring her face.

Joyce wasn't certain she wanted to continue, but she had to tell Amanda everything she knew or everything she thought she knew. If she didn't completely clear the air now she was doomed to lose her for good. She couldn't let that happen.

"What I mean is that I think I might have misinterpreted what you said at the casino. When you ran away from my house the other night, Heather said the reason why you couldn't be interested in her was because…" her voice trailed off. She couldn't finish her thought. What if Heather was wrong? What would she look like if she hinted that Amanda might be interested in her and the young woman laughed at her?

"Because of what?" Amanda prompted nervously.

Joyce took a deep breath and closed her eyes to find the courage to continue. For the sake of truth, she had to risk humiliation. "Because you might be interested in me." Her statement sounded more like a question. A weak, hopeful yet incredulous question. She opened her eyes cautiously, looking for an answer.

Amanda's blush darkened, but she remained speechless, her expression blank. Panicked, Joyce quickly added, "I know she's probably wrong, right? I mean, why would you be interested in a woman my age?" She laughed nervously. "I wanted to put it out there, because if Heather's right, then we may have more to talk about. And if she's wrong, well, at least I didn't hide anything from you and we can…"

"She's not wrong," Amanda declared, interrupting Joyce's rambling.

"What?"

"Heather's not wrong, Joyce."

Amanda's heart was pounding, her hands were sweaty, and her airways were constricting. She'd never been in this situation before. She'd never admitted her infatuation to Professor Jones back in veterinary school, and she certainly hadn't intended to admit her feelings to Joyce this morning. Forced now to make a choice between confirming or denying those feelings, however, she had to go with the truth. She'd proclaimed they couldn't have secrets from each other. Keeping the truth from Joyce now would be counterproductive. She didn't know if the feelings she had before that dinner ended so badly were damaged for good. She didn't know if she could trust Joyce again, but she knew she had to tell the truth.

"I was interested in you. I think that's why what happened at that dinner hurt so much. Being tricked into a blind date was one thing. But being tricked by the woman I thought could be the one for me was devastating." Amanda smiled to keep from crying. Joyce seemed genuinely surprised and moved by her admission.

"Oh, Amanda. If only I'd known…"

"How could you not know? Especially after what I said at the casino. I thought I'd made myself perfectly clear."

"I know. But you have to understand. I never thought for one second you could have any interest in me beside friendship. You're so young, so beautiful. It didn't even cross my mind. I fought every moment I felt attracted to you, reminding myself it was not even within the realm of possibilities."

Amanda didn't know how to reply, but she didn't want the conversation to end. They were finally getting somewhere, throwing their truths in the air and seeing where they'd fall. It felt good. Scary, but good. She spotted a bench nearby. "Would you like to sit?"

"Yes, please," Joyce answered with a laugh. They walked to the bench and sat in silence for a minute.

"So what do we do now?" Amanda asked.

"I don't know," Joyce said. "It's up to you, Amanda. Do you think you can trust me again?"

"I'm not sure. But even if I do, where do we go from here? Do we go back to being friends? Do we start dating? I mean, do you think you could get past our age gap?"

"I'm not sure, to be honest. But I know what I'd like to do."

"And what is that?"

"I'd like to start over. I'd like for us to go out as if it was the first time, with open minds. You stay open to the possibility that I might be trustworthy," she said with a wry smile. Amanda couldn't help smiling back. "And I stay open to the possibility that this could be more than friendship," she added with a more serious expression, biting at her lower lip.

Amanda swallowed with difficulty. "That sounds fair."

"I'm glad you think so." They stood and started walking back toward Amanda's condominium complex. When they stopped in front of the door, Joyce thanked her for agreeing to meet with her and hugged her. Amanda tensed up at the embrace, but relaxed when Joyce tightened her hold and cradled her chin into Amanda's neck. It was a new kind of hug, much more intimate, and a delightful way to begin the do-over Joyce had suggested.

CHAPTER TWENTY-TWO

"Are you expecting me to be happy for you? I was there when she broke your heart, remember?"

Doug stirred milk into his coffee with a spoon and dropped it in the sink. Amanda thought, not for the first time, that it wouldn't take much more effort to place his spoon in the dishwasher the break room of the clinic was equipped with, but she didn't mention it. She was used to filling the dishwasher with the dishes every other employee casually left in the sink. Beside, now was not the moment to discuss dishes. She'd told Doug that she couldn't go to his house for dinner on Thursday night because she had plans with Joyce.

"You don't have to be happy for me, but I hope you can respect my decision. I found out there were misunderstandings and insecurities on both sides and Joyce is genuinely sorry for what she did."

"Of course she is," Doug spewed. He took his coffee and left the break room, shaking his head. Amanda had never seen him this angry. Or perhaps it was disappointment more than anger. Either way he would have to come around because she wouldn't go back on her decision to give Joyce a second chance. She believed Joyce understood tricking her into a blind date was wrong but more than anything she realized she would not have done it if she could have seen past her own insecurities. If she'd thought that Amanda might be attracted to her despite their age difference, she would have acted differently.

Joyce's apology had meant a lot. But it was the way she'd hinted that Amanda's feelings could have been reciprocated if she'd been open to the possibility that convinced her to accept her proposition to start over. She'd admitted that she'd fought her attraction to Amanda every step of the way, but what Amanda hung on to was the fact that there *was* an attraction. She couldn't pass up the opportunity to see what she might do now that she was aware her age didn't matter, now that their intentions were clear. No more games. She would remain cautious, of course. But she had to try.

* * *

"Am I supposed to be happy for you? Because I can't be. To be quite honest I worry about your sanity. You're heading straight to a heartbreak, or ridicule, and I don't know which is worse. Before, you had innocence on your side. You didn't know Amanda was into you. Now you know where this is going, and you consciously choose to keep going. It's like driving straight into a concrete wall. Pure madness, Joy, completely insane. Please tell me you see that."

Barbara took a large gulp of wine. She was furious. Joyce had served her sister a glass of white wine on the patio, hoping the fresh air and the view would soften the impact of her announcement. Despite her efforts, Barbara had exploded as soon as Joyce had told her she'd convinced Amanda to see her again. She hadn't even mentioned she was considering dating the younger woman.

Joyce sighed before she spoke in a calm tone. "I wish I could tell you I don't care if you're happy for me, but it wouldn't be true. As much as I've fought it recently, I see now that your opinion will always matter to me, Barb."

"At last!" Barbara shouted out. "You're finally making sense. So tell me you're going to cancel your plans with Amanda and forget about her."

"I'm not done. Your opinion will always matter to me, yes, but what has changed is that I will never let it matter more than my own opinion. I'm sad and sorry you can't be happy for me, but I won't let that stop me from seeing Amanda. Even if our relationship might eventually go beyond friendship. Even if you worry about what people will think about me or what they'll think about you. It matters to me that you can't support me. It hurts me, but it won't stop me."

"You've lost your mind. You've been acting weird ever since Evelyn died, but now you've done it. You've completely lost your mind."

"No, Barb. On the contrary, I finally have a mind of my own."

"She could be your daughter, Joy! Do you not see how ridiculous this is?"

"I know how old she is. Our age gap doesn't matter to her. And to be honest, I'm not sure how much it matters to me yet. I'll let you know when I find out. I'm sure of one thing though: you won't decide for me."

"Oh my god, what do I have to do to get through to you?" Barbara stood up and faced Joyce, who remained calmly in her chaise lounge. "How can I make you see you're acting like a fool?" she asked through clenched teeth as she waved her arms in front of her as if she were physically shaking Joyce.

"Nothing," Joyce answered composedly. "You might as well give up right now, because nothing you'll say will make me change my mind. I'm going out with Amanda tomorrow."

"For god's sake, wake up! You're so fucking infuriating. I'm calling Heather right now," she said as she took her phone out of her purse and started dialing. "Maybe if it comes from someone Amanda's age, you'll see the light."

"I'm not convinced Heather shares your opinion, but even if she did, she couldn't make me change my mind either."

"Voice mail," Barbara announced as if she hadn't heard a word Joyce had said. "Heather, it's your mom. Call me back, we have a crisis." Joyce chuckled at Barbara's dramatic message. "There's nothing funny about this. I'm going home now because there's obviously nothing I can say or do to reach you in that kooky bubble of yours, but this isn't over. Trust me."

Joyce laughed again and watched as Barbara emptied her glass of wine and left without saying goodbye. Once she was left alone, she replayed Barbara's warning in her mind. The truth was that she was terrified that Barbara was right, but she'd promised herself and Amanda she'd keep an open mind and she would keep that promise. She picked up Barbara's empty glass and finished her own before she went back inside, followed by Dingo, who'd been hiding under her chaise lounge.

CHAPTER TWENTY-THREE

Amanda suggested the Lumber Lounge Restaurant because it was her favorite place to eat in Bangor. Although she loved being pushed outside of her comfort zone when she went out with Joyce, she figured this dinner would be awkward and nerve-wracking enough without choosing an environment that made her feel even more uncomfortable. The Lumber Lounge was a perfect mix of the comfy warmth of a ski chalet and the elegance of a fancy restaurant. Wood floors and furniture met industrial architectural elements such as steel shelving behind the white marble bar. Amanda had been relieved when Joyce had mentioned the restaurant was among her favorites as well.

Amanda waited for Joyce in front of the restaurant. She was anxious but also excited about having dinner with her. She wasn't sure what they could safely talk about without awakening recent wounds or insecurities. It was close to walking on eggshells, but she preferred that to the minefield they'd been navigating before their last talk. At least now they could see the eggshells as they moved forward.

Amanda studied her reflection in the restaurant window, swiping some lint off her sweater. She'd decided to wear charcoal pants with a button-down shirt in the same color and a black cashmere sweater over it. It was much more formal than her usual look, but she liked it. She had to admit it gave her a little more confidence. She'd considered wearing her hair down but in the end she'd pulled it back in her familiar ponytail. She was even happier she'd chosen formal apparel when she saw Joyce walk toward her, wearing a fitted black dress with a black and white silk scarf. She was stunning. Amanda couldn't help returning her smile as she approached and spontaneously hugged her.

"I hope I didn't keep you waiting too long."

"Just a few minutes, but I was early," Amanda answered as she opened the door and held it for Joyce.

The restaurant hostess showed them to their table and handed them menus, which gave them their first topic of conversation. They found out they were both fans of the chef's crab cakes and crispy calamari and ordered both to share. Joyce also ordered a glass of wine, but Amanda preferred sparkling water. She couldn't afford to have any of her faculties diminished by alcohol. She needed to remain alert.

Once they closed their menus they became quiet. Silence, which had never been awkward between them before, was now filled with tangible pressure, fear, and expectations. She went in with a safe question, "So how's Dingo?"

"Oh, he's doing great," Joyce hurried to answer, obviously relieved to speak again. "I have to confess that he's probably running more than you'd want him to, but I haven't let him jump on or off furniture yet. And he's still sleeping in his crate, despite a temporary relapse a few days ago when he spent one night in bed with me."

Amanda laughed, glad to see Joyce's playful nature again. "Running is fine. After tomorrow's appointment he won't be wearing a bandage anymore, after all. He's almost back to normal."

"That he is. Thanks to you," Joyce said with an intense gaze that expressed all of her gratitude.

"I'm glad I could help. I know how much he means to you." Joyce kept staring at her as if she were trying to communicate her deepest thoughts through her gray eyes. She held the powerful gaze as long as she could but eventually had to lighten up the mood so she could breathe again. "You know what I've been wondering since that first day at the clinic?"

"What is that?" Joyce prompted before she took a sip of wine.

"Why did you name him Dingo?"

Joyce laughed and Amanda was satisfied with the lighter tone she'd given their exchange. "That's because of my obsession with Australia," she answered.

"Really? But you do know basenjis come from Africa, right?"

"Yes, of course, I do know, but I don't care. To me he looks like a tiny dingo so I called him Dingo. I am allowed, am I not?" Joyce closed her argument with an adorable pouting lip that made Amanda chuckle.

"Of course, you're allowed. It's a good name for him."

"See, I knew you'd agree."

"So tell me more about that obsession with Australia."

Joyce told Amanda about her fascination with a novel called *The Thorn Birds* and how it had sparked her interest for the country where the story was set. She talked about her dream to travel to Australia and Amanda instantly wanted to be part of that trip. All she knew about the country was that it was where kangaroos lived, but as she listened to her talk about its cities, its outback, its history, she wanted to know so much more. Joyce's passion was contagious.

Their food arrived and they shared it with enthusiasm. They kept talking about Australia and other places they'd like to see such as Ireland and Italy. They ordered a piece of chocolate cake to share with lattes and kept talking. Amanda was relieved; she'd never expected their conversation could flow so easily again. They hadn't mentioned the dinner at Joyce's house.

They hadn't touched deeper and more sensitive topics like her childhood and Joyce's marriage to Evelyn. They were having the type of conversation Amanda imagined was appropriate for a first date. The realization gave her chills. That do-over Joyce had suggested might very well work after all, she mused.

After dinner, Amanda refused Joyce's offer to drive her home. She needed the short walk to reflect on the evening and revel in her complete satisfaction. She walked Joyce to her car and was both surprised and ecstatic when Joyce held her hand as they made their way through the parking lot. The touch was almost overwhelmingly pleasurable. She'd never held hands with a woman before, not like this, and she couldn't believe how much sensation could channel through the skin of her palm and fingers.

"I had a lovely time," Joyce said when they got to her car. She turned to face Amanda without letting go of her hand.

"So did I."

"Enough to do it again? Saturday?"

"Enough to do that, yes," Amanda answered absently, distracted by the caress of her fingers in the palm of her hand.

"Great. I'll see you at the clinic tomorrow," Joyce announced before she dropped her hand to hug her.

Amanda watched Joyce get behind the wheel and drive away. She placed her hands in her pockets and started walking home. She closed the hand Joyce had been holding into a fist, as if she could trap the feeling of Joyce's fingers within it. Somehow it must have worked, because she still felt the touch of Joyce's hand on hers when she got to Franklin Street.

CHAPTER TWENTY-FOUR

Joyce arrived at the clinic early for her appointment with Dingo. She sat with the dog on her lap and tried to control the silly grin on her face. The attempt was futile. She'd gone to sleep with thoughts of Amanda and she couldn't wait to see her. Their interaction had been so easy and natural over dinner last night. The evening had proven to her that she'd been right to fight for her forgiveness. It had also allowed her to believe a romantic relationship with the younger woman might not be so absurd after all. Holding her hand had been purely instinctive and she hadn't fought it. It felt right.

Kissing her had seemed as appropriate in the moment, but she'd stopped herself, although she still couldn't figure out how she'd managed to do so. She'd stared at Amanda's full lips with a hunger she hadn't experienced in years. She'd wanted to taste those lips even more than she'd wanted to that night in her art studio, but her intuition had told her to wait. She wanted to make sure she didn't rush anything. It might make their progress excruciatingly slow, but having to take a step back would be much worse. It seemed to be working. Some twelve hours had passed since their dinner and she could honestly say she didn't regret holding Amanda's hand. She couldn't wait to do it again. That was something.

Setting the pace was new to her, but she found she was enjoying doing so after following Evelyn's lead for twenty-eight years. It was a responsibility she took very seriously, knowing that Amanda's anxiety and lack of experience would keep her from initiating the first caress, the first kiss, or the first anything. She promised herself to always keep that in mind.

When Doug Perry showed up in the reception area and started talking with the lady behind the desk, she smiled at him timidly. She was still embarrassed by the scene she'd caused the last time she'd been in his presence. Instead of returning her smile, he glared at her with disdain and turned his back to her. Obviously, he wasn't ready to forgive her behavior.

Or perhaps he disapproved of her relationship with Amanda. If so, he wouldn't be the only one. She started wondering if anyone had seen her holding Amanda's hand last night. The thought tied her stomach into knots. Feeling sick, she closed her eyes and took a deep breath. The fact that other people's opinions affected her this way was another reason to take things slow with Amanda. If a simple glare from Doug Perry was enough to almost make her wish she hadn't held her hand, she'd been right not to kiss her. She had to get this indecisive bullshit under control before she could move forward. Amanda deserved more than a wishy-washy woman by her side.

"Ms. Allen, we're ready for Dingo," Isabelle announced.

"Good. I'll follow you."

Joyce took Dingo in her arms and carried him to the exam room. He could have walked, but holding him comforted her and she didn't want to appear upset when she saw Amanda. She shouldn't have worried because as soon as Amanda entered the exam room, the knots in her stomach disappeared and she felt her mouth shape into the silly grin she'd temporarily lost. Amanda wore a similar expression, the light in her eyes betraying her excitement.

"Hi," the veterinarian said softly.

"Hello," Joyce answered in the same foolish, adolescent intonation.

Amanda cleared her throat and when she spoke again she'd found at least some of the professional tone she clearly wanted to maintain in Isabelle's presence, "So, today's the day," she started as she brought her attention to Dingo, who was standing on the exam table. "We'll remove Dingo's soft bandage and we'll send him home without any bandage. Still no jumping for the next two weeks, which will be a lot more difficult to control without a bandage. Then one last visit with me to take X-rays and confirm he's back to normal. How does that sound?"

"It sounds perfect. We'll both be happy to be back to normal. We can't wait to go out hiking with a good friend of ours. Right, Dingo?"

Joyce enjoyed seeing the blush on Amanda's face and found it difficult not to chuckle. Amanda cleared her throat again. "Well, you'll be able to do that very soon. You have the scissors, Isabelle?"

"Yes, right here."

Joyce watched quietly as Amanda and Isabelle freed Dingo of his soft bandage. The dog lay obediently on his side as they cut through the multiple layers of cotton wadding and soon his leg was uncovered. The odor was not nearly as bad as it had been the first time they'd removed his bandage, but the sores were still there. His leg also appeared smaller than his other back leg, probably because the hair that had been shaven had not grown back yet. "He looks a little funny," she said, making both Amanda and Isabelle giggle.

"He will for a while, I'm afraid, but give it a month and it will be like nothing ever happened. Trust me," Amanda offered.

"I do," Joyce answered truthfully, causing another blush on Amanda's freckled cheeks.

"Good. Okay, so we'll go get him clean now. I assume you want to wait."

"You know I do," Joyce confirmed.

"Yeah, I figured. Isabelle will come get you in the waiting room when we're ready."

Joyce hoped Amanda would send Isabelle ahead with Dingo. She desperately wanted a moment alone with her, to tell her how much she'd enjoyed their evening together or to hold her hand again for a few seconds. But Amanda followed Isabelle and Dingo and she was left alone in the exam room. She sighed dramatically and went to sit in the waiting room, where she daydreamed about Amanda until Isabelle came to get her again.

Amanda and Dingo were already in the exam room when Joyce entered. "Well, we officially have a clean, bandage-free Dingo here," Amanda announced gleefully as Dingo wagged his tail with enthusiasm.

"Wonderful," Joyce exclaimed.

"We'll get you an antibiotic cream for the sores on his leg. Apply it generously every morning and every night. You'll see that they'll heal very quickly now that his leg isn't covered with a bandage anymore."

"That's good to hear." Joyce would be happy to see those sores go away.

"Now for the not-so-happy part of the news," Amanda started as she wrinkled her nose.

"What?" Joyce asked with apprehension.

"Well, Dingo has full access to his leg now and the sores will be crazy itchy while they heal so he'll want to lick them."

"Oh no, I see where this is going. That damn plastic cone will have to be over his head at all times, right?"

"I'm afraid so. At least until he doesn't try to lick his leg anymore." Dingo started frenetically licking one spot on his leg, as if underscoring Amanda's point.

"I get the idea," Joyce granted. She grabbed Dingo's face and physically kept him from licking his leg. "I have one at home, but I think he'll chew through to the bone by the time I get home if we don't put one on him right away."

Amanda and Isabelle chuckled. "Isabelle, would you go get us an Elizabethan collar, please?"

"Sure," the vet tech agreed.

Isabelle left the room and Joyce cursed the fact that she had to hold Dingo's face with both hands and miss her chance to touch Amanda. At least she could talk. "I really enjoyed our time last night. I can't wait for tomorrow," she whispered in that same silly tone she'd said hello earlier.

"Same here," Amanda murmured back. She leaned against the table and brought one hand to Dingo's neck, caressing him before she rested her hand on Joyce's. The contact was delightful and appeasing. "Do you have any idea what you want to do?"

Do I ever, Joyce thought. She shook those thoughts away. "I figured we could go for a walk in your neighborhood, stop by the museum or any of the small shops around there if we feel like it. I just want to spend time with you."

"That sounds lovely." Amanda dared to caress the back of Joyce's hand with her index finger.

"Mhm," Joyce agreed, closing her eyes to better enjoy the touch of Amanda's finger. "I'll meet you in front of your building around one?"

"Perfect," Amanda answered before Isabelle came back with the collar she'd requested. They struggled to adjust the plastic device around Dingo's neck, laughing more than the situation justified. Joyce simply couldn't help her laughter. Her heart was overflowing with joy that needed to be expressed and laughter was the most natural way for it to come out. She imagined Amanda's laughter came from the same place. Isabelle's giggling, however, probably came from her amusement at their behavior. Joyce truly didn't care.

CHAPTER TWENTY-FIVE

Amanda was still feeling giddy on her walk back home that Friday. She'd been floating all day long after Joyce had left the clinic with Dingo. She'd ignored Doug's reproachful looks. She was happy. Sooner or later he would see that and accept it. If he didn't, then he wasn't the friend she thought he was. She'd managed this long without friends and she could do it again if she had to. She liked Doug, but if she had to choose between him and Joyce, the choice was clear.

Remembering that her fridge was empty, she decided to grab dinner to-go at the Bagel Café before she went home. She'd already ordered her turkey, cream cheese, baby spinach, and tomato sandwich when she spotted them, or she would have turned around and left before they could see her. Barbara and Heather were sitting at a table close to the front windows.

Amanda stood at the counter with her back to them, waiting impatiently for her sandwich, praying it would arrive before they noticed her. When she risked a glance in their direction again, however, Heather was looking at her with a friendly smile and waved. She was waving politely back when Barbara turned around and noticed her.

The young woman on the other side of the counter handed Amanda a brown paper bag and she headed for the door only to hear Barbara's dictatorial voice call out to her. "Amanda, please come and join us for a minute." She felt trapped.

She grunted internally and reluctantly made her way to the table but didn't sit, holding her paper bag with closed fists. "I can't stay, but I hope you have a pleasant evening."

"Sit down for a minute, young lady, before you run away again. I'm beginning to think it's me you're running from," Barbara said with a loud, obnoxious laugh.

"Mom," Heather pleaded, "if Amanda says she can't stay, let her go." Heather then turned to her, "I'm really sorry about what happened the other night. I, for one, think you and my aunt would make a great couple. Don't listen to anything my mother says."

"Shut up, Heather. A great couple? You can't be serious. But of course, I should have known you would encourage your aunt's ludicrous behavior."

Amanda watched as mother and daughter argued, thinking she should probably make her escape, when Barbara looked up to her, "You realize my sister will be eligible for Social Security before you reach forty, right? Think about it, Amanda, and get out of this before it's too late. Before you cause Joyce and yourself more pain."

Amanda wanted desperately to find a witty comeback, but nothing came. "Barbara, Heather, it was lovely to see you. Good night," she simply said. Then she smiled, turned around, and walked out of the restaurant as calmly as she could. As soon as the door closed behind her, she quickened her pace and by the time she reached Norumbega Parkway, she was practically running. Certain they could no longer see her, she slowed down and took a few deep breaths to calm herself.

She couldn't believe how snooty Barbara could be. She vowed not to let her words get to her. She couldn't help but feel compassion for Joyce though. With a sister like Barbara, it wasn't surprising that she'd been so insecure about their age difference. She could only hope Joyce would somehow break free of the severe judgment she'd been subjected to all her life.

CHAPTER TWENTY-SIX

Joyce and Amanda walked down Central Street to Main Street at a leisurely pace. They didn't talk much. They didn't even stop to visit any of the shops inside the red brick buildings decorated with beautiful arched windows that lined up the sidewalk. They just walked as closely as they could without holding hands. Joyce desperately wanted to but would never dare on such a busy street in bright daylight. Instead, every time their arms accidently rubbed against each other, she took pleasure in the sensation of Amanda's sweater against skin left bare by the sleeveless top she was wearing. She often glanced at Amanda, who met her gaze every time. The moment was almost magical.

Then the beautiful, blue mid-September sky they'd walked under quickly filled with dark clouds and rain started falling with the same intensity with which the sun had been beaming a few minutes earlier. Joyce and Amanda laughed as they rushed inside the first store they could reach, a nearby candy store.

"It must be fate," Amanda said with the excitement of a child in…well, in a candy store. Joyce watched with amusement as Amanda, eyes wide open, took in the colorful sight of sweets all around them. Hard candy, lollipops, caramel, toffee, chocolate, truffles, the options were endless. The aromas that filled the air were mouth-watering. Anyone with a sweet tooth would find bliss in this shop, and Amanda obviously was among them.

"Pick something. Anything. I want to treat you to your favorite," Joyce offered enthusiastically.

"Okay, but it will be hard to decide."

"Take your time. We can't go anywhere while it's raining anyway."

Joyce followed Amanda to each of the candy displays placed all around the store. She walked close behind her and breathed in the smell of fresh rain on her red hair. While the array of sweets that had Amanda so excited left Joyce almost indifferent, she salivated at the thought of kissing the neck exposed by her ponytail.

"I saw your sister and your niece last night," Amanda revealed as she stood in front of a display showcasing homemade fudge.

"Oh?" Joyce simply asked, abruptly awakened from her own sweet fantasy.

"Yeah. They were at the Bagel Café when I stopped by to get dinner."

Before she realized what she was doing, Joyce took a step back to put some distance between her and Amanda, the mere mention of her sister's name sufficing to make her more self-conscious. She'd been entirely focused on Amanda before, but now found herself looking around the store to check if she spotted any familiar faces. She hated herself for it. "Did they say anything to you?"

"Yes. They said hi, of course."

"Of course," she repeated cautiously, hoping Barbara hadn't said anything else but knowing her sister well enough to realize her hope was delusory.

"And then your sister said I should put an end to our relationship before we get hurt. Something along those lines, anyway. I can't remember exactly. Our age difference really bothers her, doesn't it?"

"Yes, it does," Joyce confirmed with a deep sigh.

"Is that why it bothers you so much?"

She sighed again, wondering how the conversation had turned so serious so quickly. "I think so. I'm not certain. It doesn't help, that's for sure."

"That's what I figured," Amanda said casually. She walked back to the section where they'd seen gourmet chocolate truffles and Joyce followed. "Personally, I don't care what your sister thinks. You should know that. Your age doesn't matter to me. I understand it's not that easy for you to discard your sister's opinion, but I really hope you can find a way to do it."

"So do I. I'm really trying."

"Good."

"Good?"

"Yeah, good. What more can I ask for? Besides chocolate truffles, that is."

She grinned and Joyce couldn't help but smile back. The simplicity and the absence of pressure in her attitude were so refreshing and so exactly what she needed. She put enough pressure on herself. Amanda's unconditional support was a blessing. "Truffles, huh? Are you sure that's what you really want?"

"Yes. Everything else looks delicious, but these chocolate truffles are the only things I can't live without today."

Joyce chuckled. "Well, that settles it, then, doesn't it?"

They ordered a box of four truffles and Amanda insisted that Joyce select one of them. The rain subsided soon after Joyce paid for the chocolate creations and they headed back toward Amanda's condo. They'd barely made it to Franklin Street before the rain started again and Amanda invited her inside. She briefly hesitated before she accepted the invitation, wanting to spend more time with Amanda and to see her personal space.

"Coffee?" Amanda offered as Joyce looked around her open concept kitchen and living room. No one else had seen her condo yet and she wished she'd put more time into decorating it now that Joyce was observing its bare walls.

"Yes, thank you."

Amanda filled the coffee machine with water and ground coffee and pressed the start button while she kept an eye on Joyce's every move. "I haven't put much thought into decorating it yet," she felt obligated to explain.

"It's lovely as it is. Uncluttered, open. I love it."

"Really?"

"Yes, really. Your furniture looks great in the space. You could use one or two strategically placed pieces of artwork, maybe, but that's all."

"Thank you. But speaking of artwork, maybe you can help me decide where to hang Dingo's portrait. I can't decide by myself. It's on my dresser right now, leaning against the wall, but I'd like to hang it somewhere."

"Sure, I can help you with that. But don't feel like you have to hang it because I painted it."

"I don't. I really want to hang it. Milk?" She poured coffee in two large coffee mugs and started pouring milk in her own.

"Yes, please."

Amanda poured milk in the second coffee mug and handed it to Joyce. "Would you like to sit on the balcony? It's my favorite place to sit. It's covered, so I can use it even when it rains."

"That sounds perfect."

Amanda grabbed the box of truffles Joyce had purchased for her at the candy store and led the way to the balcony. She placed her coffee and the small box on the bistro table and moved the two matching chairs so they could sit side by side closer to the patio door and safe from the rain that was still falling.

"Wow. This really is a nice spot. You have a great view of the stream and the smell of the rain is wonderful," Joyce declared as soon as she sat down.

They took sips of their coffee before Amanda dared to grab Joyce's hand. Joyce let out a contented sigh at the touch and Amanda felt her own smile widen. "I've wanted to do this all afternoon."

"Me too," Joyce answered with a smile.

Amanda was delighted with the way the afternoon had turned out. She'd had a great time walking with Joyce and visiting the candy store. She'd even found a way to address her meeting with Barbara and Heather. She was glad she'd found the courage to invite Joyce to her condo. She appreciated the privacy it gave them. Even if they simply kept holding hands as they were doing now, she just needed to be alone with Joyce, to share a small space with her and no one else.

They sat and watched the rain fall as they savored their coffee. Joyce let go of Amanda's hand only to caress the length of her forearm, slowly, from her wrist to the bend of her arm down to her wrist again. The sensation gave her goose bumps. It was by far the most intimate touch she'd experienced in her life, and she didn't want it to stop. She closed her eyes and focused on the tingles Joyce's fingers left behind as they traveled up and down her arm. She wanted to remember this forever.

"Aren't you going to taste one of these truffles you couldn't live without today?" Joyce whispered sensuously, the sound of her voice amplifying the feelings initiated by her fingers and sending powerful ripples of pleasure through her body.

"I'm not so sure what I can't live without anymore," she said honestly, her voice trembling.

Joyce snickered and, taking her hand from Amanda's arm, grabbed the box of chocolates from the table, breaking the spell Amanda was under. "Come on, have one. I want to watch you eat one."

"Okay." Examining the box Joyce held out to her, she picked up the dark chocolate lava cake truffle between her thumb and her index finger, put it whole in her mouth, and savored it. She hummed loudly in pure ecstasy as Joyce watched her intently, her mouth slightly open. She was obviously enjoying what she saw.

"Is it really that good?" she asked teasingly.

"Even better," Amanda answered once most of the truffle had melted in her mouth.

Joyce then took out the strawberry crème truffle she'd selected. "It does look good."

"I'm sure it won't be as good as mine because fruit and chocolate don't belong together in my opinion, but sure, go for it," Amanda said, continuing the playful banter she'd started at the store after Joyce had made her choice of truffle.

Joyce smiled, placed the entire truffle in her mouth, and moaned exaggeratedly. "Oh it's so good," she said with a hand placed in front of her mouth, still full of chocolate. "Are you sure you don't want to taste?"

Amanda glanced at the box, not understanding Joyce's question. She was certain she'd seen her place the whole truffle in her mouth, so how was she supposed to taste it? When she met Joyce's gaze again, she understood. Her gray eyes, recently filled with humor, sparkled with a new kind of light as she leaned toward Amanda.

Amanda swallowed with difficulty and focused on Joyce's mouth as she slowly closed the gap between them. When Joyce's soft lips gently pressed against hers, she was surprised by her own groan of pleasure. She'd never been kissed before. Already overpowering, her gratification skyrocketed when Joyce's lips parted and her strawberry-flavored tongue teased her mouth open. Their tongues met and entangled with sweet and smooth chocolate. It felt and tasted better than anything she'd dreamed of and she soon surprised herself by deepening the kiss. She needed more. She kept exploring Joyce's mouth long after any taste of strawberry crème truffle was gone. Joyce welcomed her eagerness, encouraging it with moans and whimpers she devoured.

When Joyce broke away from the kiss, she automatically leaned forward, reaching for her mouth again, stopping only when she realized they were both out of breath. They stared at each other as they caught their breath, smiling with satisfaction. "Thanks for sharing," she managed to say.

Joyce's low chuckle had never sounded so sexy. "Anytime."

"Like now, maybe?"

"I could handle now," Joyce replied before she pressed her lips to hers again. This time the kiss didn't start slow; it went directly to the same depth and intensity where they'd left the first one. Moans mixed with heavy breathing and soon she was overcome with a level of arousal she couldn't have envisioned. She wanted more, so much more it almost scared her, as if she'd lost control of her mind and body. Joyce pulled her lips from hers to catch her breath again, but Amanda kept kissing her skin, moving down to her neck, trying to reach under the silk scarf that was in her way. That's when she felt Joyce's hand on her chin, forcing her to tear her mouth away from the tender skin of her neck and look at her.

"What? Did I do something wrong?" she asked, panting.

"No. Of course not. But I think we probably should stop," Joyce said as she held her face with both hands, staring at her mouth. She wanted her too, Amanda was sure of it. "As much as I want this to keep going, I think we should take it one step at a time. Today, our first kiss, was a big step, don't you think?"

"Yes, you're right. It was a huge step. You don't regret it, do you?"

Joyce smiled tenderly. "No. I wanted it. I had a pretty good idea it would happen today. And I know I won't regret it. But…"

"But you might regret what could happen next if it happened right now?"

Joyce hesitated and bit her lower lip before she spoke. "Maybe. I don't know, but I don't want to risk it."

Amanda sighed deeply. She knew that Joyce having regrets later would hurt worse than stopping what they were doing now. Besides, the kisses they'd shared would easily keep her daydreaming and whistling for days, perhaps even weeks. And if she was completely honest with herself, she was a little scared of what they'd been about to do next. She had no experience and was terrified it would show. In the end she had to admit Joyce was right. "One step at a time, then?"

"Exactly. One beautiful, perfect step at a time," Joyce repeated. She brushed her lips against Amanda's so softly that they barely touched. Amanda was shocked at the power the light kiss had on her body, which was so alert the slightest caress sufficed to inflame it again. Joyce stood up and walked inside. She reluctantly followed her. They kissed again at the door and Joyce left, promising she'd call to make plans for their next date.

That night, Amanda went to bed and saw Dingo's portrait still resting on her dresser. She smiled because she knew beyond the shadow of a doubt there would be plenty more opportunities for Joyce to help her decide where to hang the painting.

CHAPTER TWENTY-SEVEN

"Janice saw you and Amanda on Main Street Saturday. She asked me who was that young woman you were standing so close to."

Joyce kept her eyes closed and held the Perfect Pose even though her yoga session had been so brutally interrupted. She knew Barbara was not dropping by on this sunny Tuesday morning to see how she was doing. They hadn't talked since she'd confronted her older sister and declared she would see Amanda whether she liked it or not. She'd known Barbara would remain silent until she found more ammunition to pursue the fight. Apparently she now had.

Joyce stood and rolled up her yoga mat. She went to the dog pen and hooked a leash to Dingo's collar. Thankfully, he hadn't tried to jump and escape from the pen yet, the Elizabethan collar limiting his movements. She and Dingo then walked past Barbara to the patio door and entered the house, followed by an irritated Barbara. "Did you hear what I said?"

"Yes, I heard you. What did you tell Janice?" she asked calmly. Janice was an old friend of Barbara's and Evelyn's. The rumor mill had obviously started and although Joyce was acting impassive in front of Barbara, the truth was that she was bothered by it, which annoyed her even more.

"I told her she was just a friend and your dog's new vet, but you know Janice. She kept hinting that the two of you looked really close. Her mind is already made up. What the hell, Joy? Couldn't you at least keep your distance in public?"

"Oh come on. It's not like we were holding hands or kissing in the middle of the street. You know as well as I do that Janice would have run her mouth even if I'd been standing three feet from Amanda. She has nothing better to do. Don't you?"

"How dare you?" Barbara hissed. "I certainly have better things to do than to defend your reputation, Joyce Allen."

"Oh please. We both know the only reputation you're really concerned with is your own. So next time you see Janice, tell her the truth. Tell her your little sister has lost her mind and you don't know what to do with her anymore. Tell her you've stopped talking to me if you want. I don't care. Do whatever you have to do to save your own fucking reputation and quit acting like you worry about mine. I don't give a crap what Janice thinks of me. Am I clear?"

"You're clearly lying, that's for sure. I don't believe a word of it. Janice was among your closest friends. She was part of the world you lived in for almost thirty years. One day you'll wake up and realize you've turned your back on all of your friends and your family, my dear sister. I only hope it won't be too late when you do. I'm done trying. Call me if you ever come to your senses."

Barbara left, slamming the front door behind her. Joyce gasped at the sound, then sighed, relieved to have been delivered from Barbara's attacks, but mostly relieved to be able to drop the act she'd been keeping up in her presence. Alone at last, she started crying quietly and walked to the leather couch where Dingo joined her and lay by her side. He wasn't supposed to jump on the furniture, but she welcomed his presence and plunged her fingers into his fur as she started sobbing with much less control.

She didn't worry about Janice. That much was true. She didn't care what Janice and the rest of her former friends thought. She *did* care about the fact that she might lose her sister though. She couldn't help it. They'd shared so much since their childhood. As much as she'd grown to hate Barbara's judgmental and snobbish ways, she still loved her. She was a bright, witty, sharp, and funny woman. Most of all she was her big sister, and she knew she would always need her in her life.

Deep down, she also had to admit she understood her concern. She knew there was more behind it than Barbara worrying about her own reputation, knew that some of her warnings came from a deep fear that Joyce might get hurt. How could she not understand that when she also fought that same fear?

She wanted to be with Amanda more than anything, but she couldn't deny that for her their age gap was a genuine, almost paralyzing threat. She'd been going back and forth between moving forward and ending everything since the last kiss they'd shared. That's why she hadn't yet called to plan their next date. Every time she picked up her cell phone she thought of her young mouth trying to kiss the skin hidden under her silk scarf. The thin, wrinkled skin she'd been covering up for years. Every time she remembered the moment that she'd felt her lips move under the light fabric, the panic that had made her put a stop to Amanda's exploration resurfaced.

Yet if she chose to move forward with her, she couldn't hide the skin of her neck forever. If they made love, Amanda would see her neck—and every other imperfection on her body that betrayed her age. She thought she didn't care about their age difference now, but she'd always seen Joyce at her best. Lying naked in bed with the younger woman would leave Joyce completely vulnerable. It would be the real, ultimate test, and she was far from convinced that Amanda wouldn't care then. More importantly, she wasn't sure she wanted to find out.

Then she thought of kissing Amanda, of caressing her and making her moan with pleasure again. She thought about holding her in her arms and letting herself love her the way she wanted to, and she picked up the phone again. Having these conflicting feelings was exhausting. She wished she could discuss them with someone, with her sister, but she couldn't. She was left alone to battle with them, and she thought she might go crazy.

CHAPTER TWENTY-EIGHT

By Wednesday night, Amanda was getting scared Joyce might never call. She sat alone on her balcony and watched the rain fall. The smell reminded her of her afternoon with Joyce. Her memories of the kisses they'd shared were still comforting, but they were becoming tainted with worry. She'd started analyzing every move and every touch, looking for something that might have upset Joyce. She cursed her lack of experience. She'd been so blinded by the pure bliss these new sensations had brought her that she'd become oblivious to Joyce's feelings and reactions. She'd clearly missed something. Or…maybe Joyce simply regretted kissing her. She was about to call her to find out when her phone rang.

"Hello," she answered with apprehension.

"Hi," Joyce started timidly. "Sorry it took so long to call."

"It's okay. I was wondering if I'd done something wrong, but I'm glad you called." She played nervously with the glass of iced tea resting on the table in front of her. She heard Joyce sigh deeply.

"You didn't do anything wrong. But I've been dealing with something, and I thought I should figure it out before I saw you again. Unfortunately, I can't. Not on my own. I think it might be easier to talk it out with you. That's what I should have done from the start, I know. But I'm learning, I swear."

Joyce's nervous chuckle was strangely comforting. It made her sound insecure, which meant she needed reassurance. She wanted to talk things through with Amanda, which meant she was open to her opinion. That was positive. Not as positive as if Joyce had called to tell her she'd missed her and needed to see her right away, of course. So, while this all was definitely a little scary, all in all it was positive. Probably.

"I'll be happy to talk it out with you, Joyce. Whatever it is. And you're right; you should never try to deal with things by yourself. Especially if they relate to us. No secrets, remember?"

"Yes, I remember. I already feel better now that I've heard your voice, actually," she said softly.

"Good," Amanda whispered.

"So will you meet me at my house tomorrow after work? I'll make dinner."

"Just for the two of us, right?"

This time Joyce's laughter was more sensuous than nervous, which made Amanda smile with pride. "Yes, I promise."

CHAPTER TWENTY-NINE

Rain continued to fall the next day so Amanda drove her car to work and to Joyce's. She didn't mind the faster means of transportation for once, eager to see Joyce again. Joyce opened the front door to let her in the house and looked over her shoulder, smiling with relief when she spotted Amanda's ten-year-old, light blue Beetle. "You do have a car, thank god. With all that rain, I was thinking I should have offered to go pick you up."

Amanda laughed. "That's nice of you, but now you know. I do have a car. I just don't use it when I don't have to."

"You're putting me to shame. I should try that with Dingo when he finally is released from his plastic cone prison."

Amanda had to laugh even harder when Dingo came to the door to greet her, and she saw how pitiful he looked. A dog wearing an Elizabethan collar at the clinic seemed natural. But somehow, the same dog wearing that collar in his own environment was completely different.

"Oh, my poor Dingo. Who did this to you?" Amanda declared with empathy as she kneeled to the floor to pet Dingo and take a closer look at his leg.

"What do you mean, who did this to him?" Joyce asked with exaggerated outrage, her hands placed firmly on her hips. "You did, Doctor Carter. You're the mean one, don't you forget. I simply follow your orders."

"Do you promise me you won't lick your leg if I remove this awful thing your mommy put on you?" Amanda asked Dingo, acting as if she hadn't heard Joyce. She giggled when she heard the dramatic huff Joyce used to express her supposed indignation.

She started to remove the Elizabethan collar and Joyce kneeled down to help. "Do you really think he's not going to lick it?"

"I checked and the sores are almost completely healed already. Obviously, you've been applying the antibiotic cream the way you were supposed to."

"I told you. I follow orders," Joyce said in a low voice that conveyed a new, much more sensual type of playfulness. Amanda felt her face heat up instantly.

"Well, good. I think it worked for Dingo. Let's try it. If we see that he still wants to lick his leg we'll put it back on."

"Okay, I trust you." They worked together to free Dingo, who fortunately ignored his leg after the collar came off. Joyce looked at her with grateful surprise.

"Let's keep an eye on him all evening, but I think it will be fine."

"Does that mean he's back to normal?"

"It looks like it, but I'd still like to see him at the clinic next Friday as planned for a thorough exam."

"Of course. You've been so good with him."

"I hope I can keep being good with him in the future, as more than a vet." The expression on Joyce's face changed at the implication.

"I do too, Amanda. Do you mind if we have a glass of wine and get this talk out of the way before dinner?"

"I'd prefer that. I'm not hungry yet and I'm anxious to find out what you need to talk about. I won't have wine though. Water will be fine."

"Okay. Will you have some iced tea at least?"

"That would be perfect."

"Great. Please make yourself comfortable in the living room. I'll be right back."

Joyce walked toward the kitchen and she went to the living room, followed by Dingo. She sat on the leather couch and picked up Dingo so he could sit by her and she could make sure he wasn't attempting to lick his leg. His presence also relaxed her. She did want to know what Joyce needed to talk to her about, but she was also extremely nervous about the conversation to come. Whatever was bothering Joyce had been serious enough to keep her from calling for several days, after all. She caressed Dingo's neck and back, knowing that she needed to remain calm for Joyce's sake. As anxious as she was about their talk, she knew it had to be worse for Joyce.

Joyce walked into the living room and handed Amanda a tall glass of iced tea before she seated herself with a goblet of white wine on the other side of Dingo and started petting him too. He didn't seem to mind the extra attention. In fact, he turned to his side to give Joyce access to his belly while Amanda continued to rub his back. They giggled at his change of position. Then Joyce took a large gulp of wine and sighed.

"Whatever it is, Joyce, you know you can tell me. Please. What is it you've been trying so hard to work out on your own?"

Joyce sighed again before she started. "It's nothing new, in a way. It's our age difference."

"Oh, no. Did Barbara get to you again?"

"No. Well, yes, but it's my own insecurities I need to talk about. I won't let Barbara keep me from seeing you, but my own doubts are what keep me awake at night. It's freaking me out."

"Okay, but why? I told you your age didn't matter to me. Don't you believe me?" She could feel panic beginning to settle in. What could she do to make Joyce understand their age gap didn't matter to her? What did she have to say for her to finally believe her?

"I believe you. I believe my age doesn't matter to you, at least not right now."

"Right now? Why would it change?" Joyce abandoned Dingo's belly, picking up her wineglass and moving her fingers nervously up and down its stem. Realizing that her questions were raising Joyce's level of anxiety, Amanda took a deep breath. "I'm sorry. I'm being defensive. I'll be quiet and listen, okay? Please explain."

Joyce nodded and took another sip of wine before she continued, staring down at her goblet. "I believe you when you say my age doesn't matter to you. I really do. But the truth is that you've always seen me with my hair and makeup done and…" She paused, cleared her throat and met Amanda's gaze, "and dressed."

Joyce's vulnerability was heartbreaking. Amanda felt moved to reassure her but remained quiet and listened instead. "When our kisses became, well, more intimate the other day at your place, when you tried to kiss my neck, I panicked. I don't wear these scarves because of the way they look," she explained as she pointed to the pink silk she wore around her neck. "I wear them because they hide my wrinkly old neck. When you kissed me there, I realized if we keep going the way we are I'll have to let you see me without it at some point. Without anything at all. What I'm trying to say is I look very different when I'm naked, Amanda, and I'm not convinced you won't care about my age when you really see it."

In the silence that followed, Joyce finished her glass of wine and set it down. "So I guess that's it. I want us to move forward. I really do. I love kissing you and I feel good with you. But I'm scared. I'm terrified I'll get hurt and that fear is holding me back. There you have it. That's what I was trying to figure out."

Amanda reached over Dingo and took Joyce's hand. She was relieved when she didn't pull away. On the contrary, she held on to her hand and moved closer to her on the couch. Amanda thought carefully about her next words. She couldn't condemn Joyce's insecurities. They were justified and trying to convince her they were not would be fruitless. Instead, she chose to come clean about her own insecurities. "You know, when you stopped me from kissing your neck, a part of me was relieved."

Joyce looked puzzled at her confession. "Really?"

"Yes. You were not the only one who was scared. You know I've never been in a relationship before. I've never made love. Hell, that was the first time I ever kissed someone. I was scared I wouldn't know what to do next. Besides, I may be younger but my body's far from perfect. I have a bit of a belly and cellulite on the back of my thighs."

Joyce started laughing out loud, shocking Amanda. She hadn't expected her to laugh as she exposed her fears and the interruption offended her. "Oh my god, I remember when I first started dating Evelyn and I was so concerned about my cellulite. If that's all I had to worry about now it would be nothing at all," she explained as she kept laughing.

Amanda pulled her hand away and protested, "I bet it was a big deal back then, though, wasn't it? I'm trying to tell you I have fears too, Joyce. You can't dismiss them any more than I can dismiss yours."

Joyce stopped laughing and reached out for her hand. She didn't resist the touch. "You're right. It was a big deal to me back then and I understand it's a big deal to you now. I'm sorry I reacted that way."

They looked at each other and slowly managed to smile, their fingers intertwined. "So what do we do now?" Joyce asked.

Amanda took a deep breath and looked her straight in the eyes. "I don't know about you, but I don't want to let my fears hold me back from this relationship. I've never met a woman like you before. I want to be with you more than anything. I can't let my lack of experience and my silly cellulite stop me. It's up to you to decide if your fear of what I'll think when I see you naked is stronger than your desire to be with me."

Joyce moved closer yet, until Dingo was squeezed between them. She almost whispered her next words. "You make it sound easy."

Amanda lowered her voice as well, trying to focus on her words as her gaze dropped to Joyce's lips. "It's not easy, but it's my choice. I can't make a choice for you, though. So what will it be?"

The answer came in a brief but firm kiss that left Amanda unfulfilled. "Right now, I think kissing you is the only choice I can make," Joyce murmured before she pressed her mouth to Amanda's again.

Amanda realized Joyce couldn't possibly have been relieved of all her insecurities yet, but they were moving in the right direction. She'd missed her lips, her tongue, her taste, more than she could express, and having feared that she might never get to enjoy them again, this kiss was a welcome surprise. Joyce's mouth became more insistent. She heard Dingo jump off the couch, which allowed Joyce to lean against her. Soon she found herself pushed against the back of the couch, Joyce's upper body pressed against hers. She focused on controlling her arousal and letting Joyce take the lead. It wasn't easy when all she wanted to do was to pull her even closer, to explore every inch of her body with her hands, but their conversation had made it clear to her Joyce needed to set the pace.

Joyce ended their passionate kiss, but Amanda still felt the weight of her body on hers when she spoke. "Thank you for understanding. I've never met anyone like you before either, Amanda. You're a beautiful, unexpected gift from life, and in case that kiss didn't make it clear, I'm choosing to fight my fears with all I've got."

"Thank you."

Joyce stood from the couch and offered her hand to Amanda to help her up. "I'm also choosing to feed you dinner before we forget. You've worked all day and you need to eat something. Let's go, young lady."

Amanda giggled and gladly followed her to the kitchen. She had to admit she was getting hungry. Dingo followed them. His leg still appeared to be dry.

After dinner, Amanda insisted on doing the dishes, refusing any help from Joyce. She argued that she had already done her part when she cooked. Joyce objected that there wasn't much cooking involved in the tandoori chicken salad she'd made, but Amanda wouldn't listen. She reluctantly sat at the breakfast bar and watched Amanda work, sipping her coffee. She'd drunk only one glass of wine during dinner and she didn't want to drink more. She preferred remaining sober.

Their dinner conversation had turned around parks Amanda wanted to visit with her and Dingo and concerts she wanted to attend with Amanda. They'd also briefly discussed Australia and she'd learned that Amanda might be interested in accompanying her. The thought of traveling with Amanda delighted her.

She was glad they'd gotten the talk about her concerns out of the way earlier. It hadn't solved everything, but it had helped tremendously. She was sincere when she'd told Amanda she wanted to fight her fears. She still thought she might run away once she saw her naked, but the possibility that she might not was worth the risk.

Their easy conversation over dinner and the kiss they'd shared before it had Joyce thinking she would know sooner than later. She couldn't resist Amanda any longer. She needed to make love to her, to feel her skin on hers. She wanted to please her. It was a desire she felt all the way to the tips of her fingers. The need to touch, to build her partner's pleasure until she reached climax. She couldn't remember the last time she'd been so driven by that urge. It was more intoxicating than any wine she'd tasted.

"Well, that's it. All clean and dry. I can put it away if you tell me where," Amanda announced.

"Not now," Joyce replied as she stood from the stool she was sitting on and walked around the breakfast bar to join Amanda. "I'll do that later. Right now all I want is to resume what we were doing before your hunger got in the way," she teased.

"Oh, it was because of my hunger, was it? I don't remember complaining or asking you to stop."

"Shh," Joyce simply said as she placed her index finger on Amanda's mouth. She loved being taller than her. It helped her be more assertive, which she was learning to enjoy. She leaned forward and replaced her finger with her mouth to kiss her thoroughly. She met no resistance when she slid her tongue into her mouth, welcomed by Amanda's own eager tongue and a deep moan that intensified Joyce's appetite and vigor. She put her arms around her waist and pulled her to her hard, at the same time feeling Amanda's hand on the back of her neck pulling with matching strength. There was no way they could stop this train now. They didn't want to and there was no reason to. She left Amanda's mouth with great difficulty to catch her breath and Amanda started kissing her nude shoulder, skipping over the spaghetti strap of her camisole only to stop at the pink silk scarf she was wearing. There they were again. It was time to face the monster.

Joyce delicately pushed Amanda away. "I'm sorry," she said quickly before trying to reach for Joyce's mouth again.

Joyce stopped her with a hand firmly placed on her chest. "No, it's okay." She took a deep breath and felt her mouth and fingers tremble apprehensively when she began removing her scarf. Slowly, she moved the light and soft fabric from around her neck, until her neck was fully exposed. She felt completely naked. Tears blurred her vision as she tried to focus on Amanda's reaction.

"You're beautiful, Joyce," she heard her whisper. "So beautiful."

"No, I'm old. You can't deny it when you see my neck."

"Shh. You're beautiful," she repeated, using the tips of her fingers to caress Joyce's neck.

Joyce closed her eyes and focused on Amanda's fingers as they moved from her shoulder up to her ear on one side, down her throat to her cleavage on the front, and back up to her jaw on the other side. The sensation was both exquisite and terrifying. In equal measures. Feeling for some reason that she should put a stop to Amanda's gentle touches, she endured the excruciating pleasure instead. When her lips soon followed almost the same exact trajectory as her fingers had, fear slowly gave in to sensuality until all Joyce was able to feel was arousal. Only then did she grab her face and force her to look into her eyes. "Come upstairs with me. Please."

"Gladly," Amanda replied with a simple nod. Joyce took her hand and guided her upstairs. A different form of anxiety lodged itself in her chest when she opened her bedroom door and pulled her inside. The only woman she'd been with in this room, in this bed, was Evelyn. She wished she'd redecorated the room or at least rearranged the furniture. Then Amanda started kissing her again and she reminded herself that she'd been sleeping alone for three years. She'd waited long enough. Surely even Evelyn would agree. She closed her eyes to chase away thoughts of Evelyn and focused on Amanda's kiss. Whether she'd waited long enough or not, she couldn't wait any longer.

She pushed Amanda onto the bed until she was sitting on the mattress. She was intimidated by her youth but still wanted nothing more than to feast her eyes on it. She grabbed the bottom of her gray sweater and pulled it over her head. Underneath it, Amanda was wearing a fitted tank top. Joyce stopped to admire her, realizing she'd never really seen her figure before, hidden as it had been under ample sweaters. Her breasts were larger than she'd imagined.

"You're gorgeous," she murmured, looking up to meet Amanda's gaze. She appeared embarrassed, self-conscious. Recognizing how much the young woman was affected by her own insecurities, she resolved to be more sensitive. But…she needed to see more of her.

"May I?" she asked as she slid her fingers under the hem of the light gray top. Amanda nodded with hesitation. She moved to pull the garment over Amanda's head, gasping when she saw she didn't wear a bra. Her breasts looked as round, firm, and perfect as they'd looked in her tank top. She did have a small, adorable belly, but she was so damn beautiful. No flabby skin anywhere.

"You're so fucking gorgeous, you take my breath away," Joyce said as she pushed her on her back. Removing her dark-framed glasses and setting them on the nightstand, Amanda placed her hands on the back of Joyce's neck. Her kiss was hungry but a little more hesitant than before. She was obviously nervous, but she was still offering herself to Joyce.

The kiss deepened as Joyce took one breast in her hand. She hummed at its tautness. Amanda's moan was even louder, however, reminding Joyce that she was the first person to touch her breasts in such an intimate way. She moved her hand in delicate circles over the sensitive skin, played gently with an erect nipple. Amanda trembled under her touch and, panting, soon had to end their kiss.

Joyce watched her take pleasure in every touch, realizing that she would be the first person to give this amazing young woman an orgasm. The thought was overwhelming. It was a great responsibility, a deed more important than any doubts she had about her own body. She was Amanda's first lover and she focused all of her thoughts and energy on being the best she'd ever have. She deserved nothing less.

Joyce smiled at Amanda's face, contorted with pleasure. Then, lowering her mouth to her neck, she kissed her way to the breasts she'd been caressing. When she took one nipple into her mouth, Amanda's entire body twitched. Joyce waited for it to pass before she licked the hard nipple softly. Another strong spasm followed, accompanied by a loud gasp. Joyce waited again, amazed and thrilled to find that she was so responsive. She took her time kissing, licking, loving her breasts until the sensations became more familiar to Amanda and her body settled in calm exhilaration.

Keeping her mouth to Amanda's breast, she risked sliding a hand down her stomach and began to unbutton her jeans. Amanda jerked again and Joyce felt her muscles tense up. She caressed her stomach instead. Her small belly had flattened out now that she was on her back and her flesh was firm and soft. Joyce obeyed her urge to kiss that tender flesh, moving down to press her lips above Amanda's belly button before gently licking a circle around it. When her chin pushed against the black underwear the unbuttoned jeans had left exposed, Amanda gasped louder than before as she pushed her pelvis against Joyce's chin. If Amanda was still nervous, her level of arousal had obviously risen to a point where she no longer cared. She was begging Joyce to touch her there, to move to the center of her want. Joyce was happy to oblige.

She got on her knees so she could easily pull down the jeans and underwear that were in her way, meeting no resistance when she parted Amanda's legs so she could comfortably settle in between her thighs. She breathed in the smell of arousal, unique yet familiar, and lowered her mouth to Amanda's wanting sex. She meant to slowly explore every fold, but the first brush of her tongue against her clitoris precipitated a first, long overdue orgasm. She moved her mouth to her inner thigh and kissed her tenderly until the spasms subsided and her muscles relaxed. Then she focused on Amanda's sex again, loving it with her mouth, carefully penetrating it with one finger. She took her time, moving slowly and delicately, then faster and harder, until a second, more intense climax arrived in a wave of muscle contractions and a loud cry of joy.

Joyce moved up to kiss Amanda, who kept whimpering against Joyce's mouth. When she ended the kiss to look into her face, she recognized complete satisfaction in the brandy-brown eyes and smiled with pride. "That was…" Amanda's voice trailed off and she chuckled.

"That was what? Okay? Good, maybe?"

"It was beyond my wildest expectations," Amanda concluded with a wide smile before she crushed her mouth to hers for another passionate kiss. "I only hope I can do half as well," she added as she attempted to push Joyce under her.

Joyce resisted. "You don't have to worry about that now. Relax and enjoy for now."

"I won't relax until I make love to you, Joyce Allen. Please, let me love you the way you just loved me." Amanda's tone was playful, but Joyce knew she wouldn't back down. She was set on giving as much as she took. When Amanda gently pushed her down this time she accepted the invitation and lay on her back. She let her kiss her neck as she'd done in the kitchen. She enjoyed the attention but was unable to fully let her guard down. Her concerns were back in full force. Now that she'd seen all of Amanda's body, she felt more insecure than ever about her own.

She was overwhelmingly tempted to stop everything, but she'd promised Amanda she would fight her fears, so she resisted her impulse. She let her remove her camisole and she even helped her with her bra. She let her kiss her chest and tried to focus on the pleasure she wanted to take from her nipples being nibbled so tenderly, but all she could think about was how Amanda had to notice how limp and droopy her breasts were compared to her own.

Amanda's caresses were not clumsy or gauche despite the fact that this was her first time. She was doing all the right things the way she enjoyed them, yet Joyce couldn't bring her mind to the state of peace and abandon she knew she needed to reach orgasm. It wouldn't happen, she knew it, and the more she told herself she knew it, the less likely it was that it could happen. Her options were to stop Amanda or to fake her way through it.

She'd faked orgasms with Evelyn before when she couldn't put her mind at ease for a reason or another. It was easier than to hurt Evelyn's ego and endure her silent treatment for the next few days. Faking an orgasm now, however, was out of the question. That was not the way she wanted to start a sexual relationship with Amanda, and she'd promised her honesty. That left her with only one option. "Amanda," she heard herself call out before she could decide what she'd say next.

Amanda's face appeared above hers and their gazes met. The excitement and eagerness in her eyes had already been replaced with sadness. "What's wrong? Is it something I…"

"It's not you," Joyce hurried to reassure her before she could finish her sentence. "I guess I need a little more time to get these damn fears out of my mind."

Amanda sighed with what could only be frustration. "Don't I make you feel how beautiful you are to me?"

"You could tell me all night, my sweet girl, and it wouldn't change the fact that I don't believe it. I'm the problem here. I mean look at these compared to yours," she said waving her hand in front of her nude breasts. "Did you not notice the difference?"

"I didn't compare, Joyce. I was too busy enjoying yours."

Joyce laughed. She believed Amanda. She really did trust that the younger woman was not comparing and taking notes the way she'd been doing. The problem was all hers, she realized that, but she couldn't simply shake it away. Not tonight. "Do you think we could put this on hold for now?"

"Are you asking me to leave? Because if you are, I want to make it clear that I'm not the one running away after seeing you naked or half-naked anyway. All right?" Amanda's tone was playful. If she'd hurt her feelings, at least it wasn't beyond repair, which was a huge relief.

"Duly noted."

"Good."

Amanda made a move to get up, but Joyce stopped her. "I'm not asking you to leave, though."

Amanda stopped and looked at Joyce with a hopeful smile. "You're not?"

Joyce shook her head. "In fact, I'd be very happy if you spent the night. Do you like to cuddle?"

Amanda's smile widened. "I don't know yet, but we're about to find out."

CHAPTER THIRTY

When Amanda woke up the next morning, her cheek was pressed to Joyce's chest. It turned out she liked to cuddle after all. She watched the hand that was resting on Joyce's stomach move up and down with every deep, restful breath the woman took. Amanda tried hard to stay in the moment and be grateful for the fact that she'd spent the night with Joyce, holding her and being held by her. She was thankful for all of that and for the mind-blowing orgasms Joyce had given her. Not only was she not a virgin anymore, but the woman who'd taken her virginity was the woman she wanted to spend the rest of her life with.

She was blessed in more ways than she could count, yet she couldn't keep from feeling cheated because she hadn't been able to make love to Joyce the way she'd wanted to. What had happened between them was wonderful but a little too one-sided for Amanda to feel completely satisfied.

Amanda stared at the pants Joyce was still wearing and covered part of them with her nude leg, trying to eliminate the piece of fabric that remained between their skin. Time. Joyce had asked for more time. In the end, what other choice did Amanda have but to give her that? It wasn't like she could move on to someone else. She didn't want anyone but Joyce. And if all that stood in her way to get everything she wanted was waiting, she'd wait.

Amanda shifted her position over Joyce's body to take a peek at Dingo, who was still sleeping soundly in his crate by the bed. His leg looked dry, but Amanda reached down to touch it through the metal grid of the crate. "Good boy," she whispered once she was able to confirm the dog hadn't licked his leg all night even without the Elizabethan collar to keep him from doing it.

"If you wake him up, you take him out," Joyce whispered with an adorable sleepy voice as she stretched under Amanda.

"Oh, is that how it works? Already making up rules?"

"Yep. Good morning, by the way."

"Good morning, beautiful." Amanda repositioned herself so she could bring her face over Joyce's and look at her smile and her barely open eyes. They gave her such a mischievous look Amanda couldn't help but smile back. "Did you sleep well despite me apparently clinging to you all night?"

"I slept like a baby. Cling all you want. But kiss me first."

Amanda chuckled as she moved down to bring her lips to Joyce's. She meant the kiss to be brief and gentle, but the contact of their nude breasts surprised her and impelled her to deepen the kiss. Joyce's gasp as their nipples pressed together made the kiss even more intense, until Dingo interrupted them with a loud, whining plea.

"All right, I'll go out with him," Amanda announced as she got up and started looking for her clothes. Joyce had already covered her upper body with the bed sheet, hiding her own breasts even as she stared at Amanda's with such hunger. "Not fair," she commented before she put on her tank top. She stuck her tongue out and started getting into her jeans.

"Oh, come on," Joyce protested.

"Nope. Fair is fair," Amanda maintained as she buttoned up her jeans.

"All right, all right. There." Joyce lowered the sheet covering her breasts for a whole second and a half before she brought it up to her neck again. "Now your turn."

Amanda laughed but played the game and flashed Joyce, who laughed at her in turn. She proceeded to free Dingo from his crate, stealing another kiss from Joyce before she headed out of the bedroom.

"I'll start breakfast while you're out."

"Sounds good." Amanda would have preferred for Joyce to wait for her in bed so they could resume what Dingo had interrupted, but there was no point in being greedy. She was confident that they'd get back in bed together soon and that she'd get her turn to please Joyce. Time was not an obstacle. It was just, well, time.

CHAPTER THIRTY-ONE

"Does she make you happy?" On Monday morning, Doug had asked Amanda to meet him in his office after the staff meeting. They were dealing with two delicate and complicated cases at the moment and she thought he wanted to discuss them with her. They hadn't talked about anything personal since she'd decided to give Joyce another chance, and he'd made it perfectly clear he didn't approve.

His question was unexpected, but she interpreted it as some kind of olive branch. She could be wrong, of course, but she was getting better at guessing people's intentions.

"Yes, she makes me very happy. She still feels some insecurity over our age difference, but we'll get through that eventually. I'm sure of it." She looked Doug straight in the eye and waited for his reaction. His smile was tentative but honest.

"If it's what you want, I'm sure you will too."

"Really?"

"Yes, really." He cleared his throat and looked down to his feet, scratching his head. "I know I haven't been supportive of this thing between you and Joyce Allen. You know my feelings for her. But I can't take this awkwardness between us anymore. I have enough awkwardness in my life."

Doug met her gaze again and they both chuckled at his declaration. "Was that a joke, Doug?"

"Yeah, maybe. I guess so." They exchanged another laugh until Doug started scratching his head again. "But really, what I want to say is that I want to be more supportive moving forward. I think we were becoming good friends and I got in the way of that with my opinions about her. I'm sorry about that. Susan keeps telling me I have no right to judge the woman and she's right. If you love her, there has to be good in her, after all. Right?"

"Right," Amanda agreed with an encouraging smile. "There's a lot of good in her, and I'd really love for you to find that out. I'm sure you don't know the Joyce I fell in love with. Maybe we could have dinner, the four of us? You haven't seen my condo yet."

"Well, as long as she doesn't bring her snooty friends or her sister I think I could handle that," Doug replied with an uncomfortable chuckle.

"She doesn't see any of those friends anymore. And her sister doesn't talk to her since she's decided to date me."

"Are you kidding?"

"Oh no. Joyce has changed a lot since you worked with her on that charity committee, but I'd guess Barbara is probably the same woman you met back then."

"Well, that's a shame. I can't say it surprises me, but it's still a shame. Good for Joyce, though, standing up to her sister like that. You know, you might be right about her change of heart. I don't think the Joyce Allen I met in those days would have been able to do that."

"I told you. It's not easy for her, of course, but she's putting her own happiness first now. She didn't know how to do that when you met her."

"I see. Well, I'm looking forward to knowing that new version of her, then. She seems a lot more likeable than the version I met years ago."

"She's definitely very likeable," Amanda added with a wink that made Doug laugh again.

They moved on to talk business, but when Amanda left Doug's office they'd agreed to make definite plans for dinner with Joyce and Susan some time soon. As she went on to meet with her patients, Amanda felt strange about the entire meeting with Doug. Of course she was relieved and pleased with his decision to put his preconceived judgment on ice and give Joyce a chance. She was touched that he was willing to make that effort for her and for the sake of their friendship. But somehow his kindness and decency made Barbara's own small-minded stubbornness all the more terrible.

What made it worse was that although she was happy Doug had changed his mind, she didn't need his approval. He was a business partner and a friend, but his opinion of Joyce didn't really matter that much to her.

Barbara's support meant so much more than that to Joyce. She was her older sister, the woman whose opinion had always counted more than anyone else's in Joyce's life, except perhaps Evelyn's. She knew that and she couldn't help but feel guilty about receiving support she hadn't asked for while the woman she loved couldn't get the same consideration from her own sister. It wasn't fair. She hoped Barbara would come around some day. More than anything, she hoped Joyce could keep standing up to her until that day came.

CHAPTER THIRTY-TWO

Joyce and Amanda had finished doing the dishes together and were sitting on the patio, enjoying the cool of this late September evening. It was Tuesday and she hadn't seen Amanda since she'd left her house on Sunday. She'd missed her terribly. Dingo sat between their chaise lounges, but his collar was secured to a long tie-out cable. In the mere two days since Amanda had removed his Elizabethan collar, he'd quickly gone back to being the explorer he'd been before his injury and Joyce couldn't trust him not to run away.

"Dinner was delicious," Joyce announced. It had been strange to see someone other than Evelyn use the outside grill, but she imagined those awkward moments were unavoidable. She would be faced with more of them as she pursued her relationship with Amanda and she accepted that fate.

"Oh please, it was just a hot dog." Amanda giggled and pushed her glasses up the bridge of her nose with her index finger. She was beyond charming. She'd removed her sweater while she was cooking, claiming she was hot for the first time since Joyce had met her. The fitted, black V-neck T-shirt she was wearing revealed her arms and a hint of cleavage but also allowed Joyce to see the shape of her round breasts under the stretched cotton. She swallowed. She desperately wanted to make love to Amanda again. The only thing that kept her from it right now was the fear that she would want to reciprocate. Sooner or later, she would need to accept that fate as well, wouldn't she?

"It was a delicious hot dog," she replied.

"I'm glad you liked it."

"You know, what I like most is having you here with me. I don't care what or even if you cook."

"That's good to know." Amanda wrinkled her nose playfully and Joyce couldn't resist any longer. She stood from her chaise lounge and carefully stepped over Dingo to walk the short distance that separated her from Amanda's chair. Amanda moved her legs to make room for her to sit. "That's better. You were way too far away all the way over there."

"That's what I thought as well," Joyce agreed. She inclined her face closer to that of Amanda's, who quickly bridged the gap for the unchained kiss she'd been anticipating since the much more reserved kiss they'd shared at Amanda's arrival. Groaning when their tongues moved smoothly against each other, she got on her knees so she could be on top of Amanda and dictate the depth and strength of their kiss. She cupped one breast with her hand and smiled against Amanda's mouth when she heard her gasp with pleasure.

"Oh my god, it's worse than I thought."

Barbara's voice startled Joyce and she jumped to her feet. She turned to face her sister, who was standing by the patio door. Her eyes were wide open and she was shaking her head in disbelief.

"What the hell are you doing here?"

"I was checking on you to find out if you'd come to your senses yet, but I see that you've gone off the deep end instead. You look ridiculous."

"Okay, well, I guess I'll let the two of you catch up," Amanda announced as she got up from her seat. She sounded hurt, but calm. "I'll go grab my stuff."

Joyce took a hold of her hand to stop her from walking past her to the patio door. "You're not going anywhere, Amanda. You, on the other hand," she added as she walked straight to Barbara until their faces were a few inches apart and she could properly communicate the fury Barbara's intrusion and complete lack of respect had caused. "You turn around and leave right now, you hear me?" She said the words calmly but firmly, without blinking.

"You're going to kick me out, Joy? I'm your sister, remember?"

Barbara's defiant glare only made her angrier, but she took a deep breath to keep her tone level. "Damn right, I am. Last time you were here, dear sister, you said you wouldn't talk to me until I ended my relationship with Amanda. Well, I didn't. And I won't. So go. And this time I'm the one telling you to stay away unless you can accept that Amanda and I are together and you can show us the respect we deserve."

"I'll never accept that relationship. Come on, it's ludicrous. Do you hear yourself?"

"Fine. I guess we'll never talk again, then." She swallowed around the lump in her throat, but she wouldn't back down.

"Watch what you're saying, Baby Sis. You do realize you're about to break ties with your family over this…" Barbara looked at Amanda with disdain, "this kid, right?"

"I know exactly what I'm saying. This kid loves me for who I am, for everything I am, which is something you obviously can't do. I think my choice is pretty obvious. Don't you think?"

"You're so out of line, Joy. Do you think I'd care so much about your inappropriate relationship with this girl if I didn't love you?"

"If that's the only way you can love me, Barb, I don't want it. You understand? Now go. And don't come back."

"You'll regret this. Don't do it."

"I said go. Now."

Joyce opened the patio door and they walked to the front door in silence. When she opened it, Barbara hesitated. "Joy…"

"Get out."

Barbara sighed with irritation and shook her head, but finally left. Joyce closed the door and leaned against it until she heard the Mercedes' engine start and leave. She sighed with relief.

She didn't feel good about her altercation with Barbara, but she felt empowered by the direction it had taken. She hadn't suffered through her insults, waiting patiently for her to be done. She'd taken control of the conversation and had even made her own ultimatum. She'd refused to take the blame for their falling out. She'd put the responsibility on Barbara's shoulders. She wasn't doing anything wrong. She was simply in love with a younger woman. A woman who wasn't asking for anything more than to love her in return. A woman who, as she'd told Barbara, loved her for who she truly was. A woman who was waiting for her on the patio right now.

Joyce took a deep breath, filling her chest with air and the strength she'd just found out was in her. She freed her neck of the blue silk scarf she was wearing and let it drop to the floor on her way out to the patio. Amanda was sitting on her chaise lounge, petting Dingo, who lay by her side. Joyce smiled at the sight. She closed the patio door quietly and walked to Amanda, who frowned with concern.

"I'm sorry you had to go through this."

"It's not your fault," Joyce replied as she kneeled down on her chaise lounge, straddling her as she had been before they were so rudely interrupted. "And I realize it's not my fault either. What we can't do is let her ruin our evening." She bent down to kiss Amanda but was held back by firm hand on her chest.

"What if she comes back?"

"She won't. And if she does, she'll get an eyeful. Not our fault. Not our responsibility." She went for that kiss again, but Amanda's hand remained on her chest.

"What happened to your scarf?" Amanda asked in a whisper as she moved her hand from Joyce's chest to her neck and caressed it with her fingertips. Joyce felt nothing but pleasure from the touch.

"I figured I didn't need it. You do love me for all I am, right? Crepy skin and all?"

"I do. I was glad when you told your sister that. But I'm even happier you finally seem to believe it."

"Sometimes saying the words out loud makes them true. I don't know." Joyce moved closer to Amanda's ear and continued, murmuring, "All I know is that I want your hands on me. I want you to take me. I want to be yours."

Amanda whimpered and started kissing her neck. "Should we move to the bedroom?"

Joyce rose to her knees and slipped out of her sleeveless silk blouse in one easy movement before letting it fall to the ground. "No. Right here. Right now," she added as she removed her bra and sent it to the concrete patio floor with her blouse.

Her plea sufficed to convince Amanda to start kissing her nude breasts with skills that equalled her hunger. Joyce watched her nipple disappear into Amanda's mouth and her arousal reached heights she couldn't remember. She saw her move her tongue over one breast and gather the other in her hand and she didn't care about her less than optimally tight skin. Amanda was enjoying it, feasting on it, and the sight made her pant and moan with desire. She felt wetness between her legs. She needed Amanda's hand there, on her sex, inside her.

Without pushing her away from her breasts, she unbuttoned her Capri pants and took Amanda's free hand and plunged it into her underwear. "Take me," she repeated in a ragged breath. She obeyed eagerly, easily finding her wetness and her opening. Joyce felt fingers slide inside her and she gasped loudly. She started riding her hand frantically, rubbing her sex on Amanda's hand and wrist. The sensations were overwhelming. She felt perspiration on her forehead and on her chest. She breathed hard in rhythm with the waves of pleasure that rose through her until she reached climax and let her body fall onto Amanda. She gathered her in her arms and held her until she could breathe again, until she could use her muscles again and found the strength to state the obvious. "That was amazing."

"It really was," she heard a giggling Amanda answer.

Joyce lifted her head from Amanda's shoulder so she could see her. Her smile was cheerful, her eyes were sparkling. She was happy. Simply yet completely happy. "I'm so in love with you," she couldn't help but declare. There was no point keeping it in. She was undeniably in love with this young, wonderful woman. Amanda's expression changed. She looked surprised by her disclosure. Then her smile widened and tears of joy filled her eyes.

"I'm in love with you too. Thank you so much for letting me…"

"Don't thank me yet. You don't know how insatiable I am. I can't blame you, though. I didn't know it myself until now."

Amanda laughed. "I don't think that will be a problem."

Joyce kissed her, slowly pressing their lips together, marvelling at how well they fit. "Perfect. Will you please stay the night? I can drive you to your place tomorrow before work so you can change."

"I'll be happy to."

They went upstairs and set up Dingo in his crate. Joyce took off the rest of her clothes and watched Amanda undress. They climbed in bed together and made love for most of the night. Joyce let her explore all of her body. The light wasn't on, yet she felt exposed. Exposed but never judged, which allowed her to move past any hesitation.

She was Amanda's. And Amanda wanted all of her, flaws included. Her love was unconditional, unlike Barbara's. That had become evident when she'd faced Barbara earlier and decided on the spot to smash down her walls and let Amanda in once and for all. She was worth her trust. She wouldn't run away.

CHAPTER THIRTY-THREE

Joyce was surprised when she received a call from Heather on Thursday morning asking her to come to her mother's house for tea. If Barbara had called, she likely would have said no, but she was curious about Heather's choice to get involved in their disagreement. It wasn't like Heather to meddle in things that didn't concern her, which made her believe her fight with Barbara must have affected her niece in some way. She'd never seen her mother and her godmother fight seriously, after all.

Driving to Barbara's house now, Joyce felt strong enough to face anyone, including her judgmental sister. Amanda had spent the night on Tuesday and Wednesday, and she was beyond happy. Their budding relationship was proving to be tender, loving, and easy. So easy now that Joyce had let go of her insecurities, realizing that she'd been the main obstacle to her own happiness. Yes, sometimes she still wondered what she was doing with a woman young enough to be her daughter, but when she did, she shook her head and reminded herself she was doing what she needed to do to make Joyce Allen happy. At last.

She was no longer spending time and energy being a version of herself that could please her sister, her wife, or her circle of friends. She was being her true self, the Joyce Allen she'd almost forgotten. The fact that she made Amanda happy too was a welcome bonus and evidence to her that they were meant to be together.

Joyce parked her car in front of Barbara's house, looked at it, and cringed. She'd always hated her sister's house. Extravagantly large and aseptic, it completely lacked personality and could have belonged to any rich owner. Nothing in the cold stone exterior walls or in the generic landscaping gave any clue about the house's owners. The interior wouldn't help a stranger solve the puzzle either. Not even one family portrait could be found in it. Barbara rarely invited her sister there, preferring her surprise visits to Joyce's instead, and Joyce liked it that way.

She walked to the front door and rang the doorbell. Heather opened the door and invited her in before they shared a warm hug. "You look great, Aunt Joyce. Being in love suits you."

"Thank you. I feel great. Although I'm a little curious about this meeting."

"I know you must be, and you know I usually mind my own business, but I couldn't stand by and do nothing here. You've always been in my life. I've learned as much from you as I've learned from my parents. And I still need you."

"Oh, Heather, I hope you know that I will always be in your life. Even if your mother can never accept my relationship with Amanda and we can't get past this, I will always be there for you."

"I know, but I need you in my mother's life too."

Joyce raised her eyebrows to show her puzzlement. She didn't understand what Heather was saying.

"You might not know this, but you're kind of like a natural circuit breaker for my mother."

Joyce started to laugh. "What?"

"You keep her from going too far. Just by your presence. It's hard to explain but all I know is that even as a kid I could see that my mom was calmer when she was around you. Funny, easygoing. My mom's at her best when she's with you, and I'm afraid what not having you in her life might do to her. She's been wound up so tight since you started dating Amanda no one can talk to her."

"I understand, but I can't sacrifice my own happiness for her sake anymore. She's doing this to herself."

"I know. And I think she's starting to realize it too."

"Hm. Somehow I doubt that. How?"

"Are you two going to stay by the door talking about me all day?" Barbara asked as she approached them. "My lovely daughter spent the night trying to make me see the light. That's how. Now if you'll join me on the back porch for tea, we can chat a little more about what a bitch I am. Maybe once you've both emptied your bag I'll be allowed to go to sleep."

Barbara turned around to lead the way to the back of the house. Heather rolled her eyes and Joyce giggled at her niece's expression and whispered, "Well, this will be fun." Then they both followed Barbara.

Once on the porch, they sat in white rattan chairs and Heather poured tea. "I'm sorry to disappoint you, but I don't have a bag to empty. I said all I had to say," Joyce started, not sure what Barbara and Heather expected of her.

"Oh, that was just Mom playing the victim. Wasn't it, Mom? She's the one who has something to say to you," Heather replied with a stern look toward her mother.

Barbara sighed heavily. "I hadn't realized I was already at the age when the parent becomes the child. When did I become so old, sis?"

"Will you quit creating diversion? There's no age to act like a child and that's exactly what you're doing," Heather added with exasperation.

"All right, all right. Geez, I was just trying to be humorous. What's wrong with that?"

"She didn't come here to hear your bad jokes, Mom."

"Actually I'm not quite sure what I'm doing here yet," Joyce interjected, putting an end to the banter between mother and daughter.

"Fine, I'll get straight to it," Barbara started. She sat stiffly in her chair and took a deep breath. "I can't let you shut me out of your life, Joy. I need my baby sister too much. I don't like you dating a woman Heather's age, and I can't promise I'll ever like it, but if it means I can keep my relationship with you, I can promise never to comment about it again." Barbara looked at Heather, who jerked her head as if to indicate there was more to say. "Oh, and I can promise to be polite to Amanda." Barbara looked to Heather again, who smiled at her with pride.

"Are you saying all of this because Heather asked you?" Joyce couldn't help probing.

Barbara turned back to her and shook her head. "No. Heather did insist. A lot. But you know me well enough to know it wouldn't have changed anything in the end if I didn't think she's right. I can't lose you. I'm used to my baby sister seeing things my way, but I can't stop seeing you simply because you don't agree with me for the first time in your life. So what do you say?"

"Well, I really do wish you could see how good Amanda is for me, but I guess what you're offering is a beginning."

"So we're still sisters?"

Joyce chuckled, "Of course, silly. You'll always be my big sister. I have one condition, though."

"Okay," Barbara said with apprehension. "What is it?"

"Next time you stop by and I don't answer the front door, don't come in the house, even if the door is unlocked. Can you add that to your promises?"

They both laughed and Heather looked at them with perplexity. "You have my word," Barbara said through laughter mixed with tears.

CHAPTER THIRTY-FOUR

Amanda was discussing Mrs. Johnson's cat with Doug behind the reception desk when Joyce arrived with Dingo for their last Friday morning appointment. Amanda's throat tightened up at the thought and she remembered that fateful morning she'd met Ms. Allen and her basenji. She'd known back then her life wouldn't be the same, but she couldn't have imagined everything they'd go through and how happy she would be almost three months later.

"Amanda," Joyce said quietly with a nod and a smile before she turned to Doug. "Good morning, Doug." Joyce and Amanda had already exchanged their own "good mornings" earlier in Joyce's bed. Amanda felt her cheeks heat up at the memory.

"Good morning, Joyce," Doug answered. "We're looking forward to tomorrow."

"So are we." Doug and his wife were coming over to Amanda's condo for dinner, which thrilled her almost as much as it made her nervous. She wondered how long it would take before Barbara shared a meal with them in her turn. She wasn't looking forward to that meal, but she knew Joyce was. She'd been so delighted about her visit to Barbara's yesterday. It was definitely a step in the right direction. Amanda felt relieved that she wouldn't lose her sister because of her. Although she realized Barbara's attitude wasn't her fault, she couldn't help but feel responsible.

"Well, I have to get to my patient, but I hope you have a great day. See you tomorrow," Doug said as he scratched his head and turned around to leave the reception area.

"Great, see you tomorrow," Joyce answered to Doug's back. She then turned to Jacqueline. "We'll sit in the waiting room."

"Actually, Dingo can come with me, if you don't mind," Amanda offered. "I'll take him in the back for his X-rays and Isabelle will come to get you once I've looked at them. Okay?"

"Perfect," Joyce answered as she handed Dingo's lead to Amanda. Their hands brushed against each other and a wave of electricity passed through Amanda's body, the same kind of energy she'd felt the first day she'd met Joyce when they'd shaken hands. She wondered if that sensation would ever fade. She didn't think it would. It might evolve, take different forms, but it wouldn't fade.

"Let's go find out if you're all better," she said to Dingo, who obediently walked by her side.

"I hope your vet was as good as Amanda and you got better too," Joyce told the injured basset hound in the framed poster hanging on the wall in front of her. She'd spent a lot of time with that dog in the past twelve weeks. He'd become a friend of some sort. So much had happened in that time. "I bet you didn't think you'd ever see me this happy that first time we met, huh?" Joyce chuckled before she continued her conversation with the framed art. "I must say your mood hasn't changed much, though." She laughed harder.

"Are you all right, Ms. Allen?" Isabelle asked, smiling but obviously concerned.

"Oh yes. I'm great. Just talking to an old friend. You're ready for me?"

"Yes, we are, if you will follow me."

"Of course."

Joyce followed Isabelle to the exam room, but to her surprise, the young vet tech didn't stay. She simply opened the door for her and closed it behind her, leaving Joyce alone with Amanda and Dingo. Amanda was scratching Dingo's neck and whispering something in his ear. His tail was wagging frantically.

"What are you two up to?" Joyce asked.

Amanda turned to her with the widest smile, "I was telling Dingo he needs to stop frowning now that he's one hundred percent back to normal. But I guess he's stuck that way," she said through giggles as Dingo licked her cheek.

"I'm afraid he is, but will my smile do? That's such wonderful news." Joyce walked to the table and hugged Amanda. Then she grabbed Dingo's face and kissed his nose.

"I also told him we'd go on a hike this evening. It'd be the perfect way to celebrate his recovery, don't you think?"

"Absolutely," Joyce agreed. She grabbed Amanda's face in a similar way she had Dingo's and kissed her mouth. "Thank you for making him all better, Doctor Carter."

"That kiss is what I was hoping for when I asked Isabelle to give us time alone."

Joyce laughed. "Oh really? Then you might like the next kiss. This one is to thank you for making me all better too." Joyce pressed her lips to Amanda's again and wrapped her arms around her neck, pulling her tightly against her mouth. Isabelle or even Doug could walk in, she wouldn't care. All she cared about was this kiss and making sure it expressed the depth of her gratitude to Amanda. When she broke the kiss, she moved her mouth to her ear to whisper, "I love you."

"I love you too, but I don't see how I made you better," Amanda whispered back.

"You don't? You not only helped me find my true self but you showed me it was okay to be that person. That's a kind of recovery too, don't you think?"

"If that's the case then I think we both recovered with Dingo in some way. I may have helped you see it was okay to be you, but you taught me I could love another human being. That's huge."

Joyce looked into Amanda's eyes and saw them glisten with tears. "This one is to celebrate our recovery, then," she murmured against Amanda's lips before she kissed her again.

Bella Books, Inc.

Women. Books. Even Better Together.

P.O. Box 10543
Tallahassee, FL 32302

Phone: 800-729-4992
www.bellabooks.com